MW01243985

The Red Spade

To my wife, Ruth,
The love of my Life.
Someone said Ruth & Arne,
Arne & Ruth.
Alex Hunt
aka Arne Andersen

The Red Spade

Alex Hunt

Heather Publishing   UPS Box 481
Marana, Arizona 85658

This edition was prepared for publication by
Ghost River Images
5350 East Fourth Street
Tucson, Arizona 85711
www.ghostriverimages.com

ISBN 978-1-7333149-6-1

Library of Congress Control Number: 2023905581

Printed in the United States of America
April, 2023

Contents

Other Books by Alex Hunt

Who is Peter Compton?
- Political Intervention
- A Little Favor
- The Turner Incident

Political Intervention Part II
- The Mission

The Snake Pit

The Monk Stone

This book is dedicated to

My wife and best friend

On their last day,
make sure each man is given a special present:

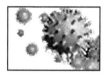

the virus

Preface

I wrote this story about three years ago, however I thought the story was too short to have it published. I tried fleshing it out and thereby make it longer. The more I wrote the more the story got diluted and I didn't recognize the point of the story. In other words it turned into gobbledygook. My wife and staunchest critic told me the original story was good and timely and to have it published.

A great portion of the story takes place in Oslo, Norway. My wife and I spent seven years in Norway after we retired. I had uncles and cousins who had been involved both in the Norwegian government and its military, so I heard what you might call sagas of how the government and its industrial complex operated.

This story is fiction based on true events. However, literary license has been taken in describing some events.

Alex Hunt

Chapter 1
Insight

"Well, how was America? We heard you came in late last night, so we decided to leave you alone; got your message that your flight was delayed." Jens Skogen, their son, took a seat at the kitchen table.

"We get a distorted view here in Norway through our news media; America is a tough modern country that can do anything."

"Did you make the rowing team?" asked his mother.

"Yes, I made it," said Jens.

"Congratulations" joined his mother and father in unison.

"What is going on in here?" It was Anna, their cook. "Welcome home, Jens. It looks like they fed you well in America. I think you have grown a few more inches and your arms and shoulders are definitely bigger. What can I get you; the usual two-boiled eggs?"

"That would be great, Anna, the rest of the food is on the table."

"Have you called Laura yet?" asked his father. "She has been over here for dinner a few times."

"No, I haven't called her yet. She made the handball team so we will both be in Tokyo next summer."

"She told us she's been driving her family nuts these past 6 months since you've been training in America. I can't see how she could miss you; you two have been talking on the phone every day. I know cause I've been paying your cell phone bill," said his father smiling.

"Here are your eggs, Jens. Good to have you back home."

"Thanks, Anna; how is John?"

"He's fine; has been a little grumpy the last few days which means I haven't been taking care of his needs, which I intend to do tonight. We are heading up to Little Hammer tomorrow to do some cross-country skiing, so he'll be back to his old self."

"Don't take all the starch out of him, Anna, he is in his 50's now, go easy on him."

"Listen to who is giving me advice; poor Laura won't be able to walk after tonight or tomorrow. Take your own advice."

"Your father and I are taking the train up to Voss today to the Fleisher Hotel for the yearly smoked sheep's head celebration and will be back sometime Monday. Anna is off until Tuesday so you and Laura have the whole house to yourself for the next 4 days."

"Not to change the subject, but how are the factories going, Dad?"

"Fine, Henrik rewrote the production program. You know he was offered a scholarship to do his Master's Degree when he was over at MIT, but he didn't care for the atmosphere there; too much back stabbing and not enough teamwork. I have him on a salary; wouldn't take a bonus for the new program, so I bought him a new car; kept it in the company name so he wouldn't have to pay taxes on it. I kept asking him what kind of car he liked but he wouldn't tell me so I asked Laura, being his sister. if she knew. So now he drives around in a new Volvo SUV with all the bells and whistles instead of that wreck he had."

"Wreck is right; did you know it had a large hole in the floor? Henrik said it was a new kind of air conditioner. That was nice of you, Dad, he is not only my best friend but also the best computer person I know."

"By the way, have you had any problems with your computer? I turned mine on last night but couldn't get it up; this morning I had messages and programs on it like it had been hacked. I'm going to get Henrik over here as soon as I can; he definitely needs to check it out."

"We haven't had any problems; your mother is into ancestry, so she is the one that's using it."

"Well, I better get him; you two have a good time, and Mom, don't make too many demands on Dad, he looks tired; let him relax a little."

"I knew the time would come when my son would give me advice on how to spend a few days with my husband, but I didn't think it would come so soon."

"Behave yourselves," said Jens as he got up from the table and headed upstairs to his room. He called Henrik and explained his problem. Henrik asked if he could come over now because he had to be somewhere later-on and could he bring his sister Laura over – she was driving him nuts. Come on over had been Jens' reply.

Jens was looking down from his window as Henrik pulled up the driveway in a beautiful new car. Henrik came up first.

"I see you have a new car," said Jens shaking Henrik's hand.

"Yes, a very nice person bought it for me. I don't know how to properly thank him for it."

"I think you already have. Where is Laura? I saw her come

in with you."

"She's downstairs talking to Anna. She will be up in a few minutes." Jens explained the problem with his computer. Henrik sat down and started pressing some keys. "Give me your password." Henrik typed it in and waited. "Hey, you have a friend here; let's see what he has to say. The date time group indicates his last transmission was 3 days ago. He will contact you again on Sunday, December 1, 2019 at 1:00pm. He says to press the printer key; he has numerous pages for you to look at."

"The printer is on," said Jens.

The printer started spitting out pages. "Your friend's call sign is *The Red Spade*, spade as in shovel."

"Where is he located?"

"Shanghai, China; who do you know there?"

"I have no idea. The only Chinese person I know was a student at the University here in Oslo. He was here for a year and I think I only spoke to him about a dozen times. He was interested in our rowing club and watched us practice. He seemed nice; was tall for a Chinese, at least from what my perspective is regarding Chinese."

"Do you remember his name?"

"No, but I could find out from the University."

"Well, you have pages of text from him. Listen Jens, your computer is fine and I have to go. Kirsten is waiting for me so if you have any problems, let me know and I will be here December 1st at 1:00pm."

"Thanks, Henrik."

Laura walked into the room and hugged Jens and gave him a soft kiss on the lips. "Welcome home, Jens; I have missed you."

"Well, from that kiss I don't think you have missed me too much; where were you? I heard you walk in with your brother."

"I've had a long talk with Anna and believe me, you will be happy when I'm through with you."

"Anna is dangerous; don't believe everything she says."

"Are we alone or is my brother coming back?"

"He won't be back unless I get bored; by the way, you look great, Laura."

"How can you tell? I still have my clothes on."

"Oh! that kind of Anna talk." Jens took her in his arms and kissed her long and soft.

"God Jens, you feel strong and in good shape."

"How can you tell? I still have my clothes on."

"Not for long." Laura started undressing Jens and told him to lay down on the bed. She also undressed and joined him stating that *she was in charge.*

"Just don't hurt me," said Jens laughing as he pulled her to him.

Afterwards Laura fell asleep with her head on his shoulder. She woke and went into the bathroom. When she returned, she sat on the bed looking at him saying, "That was the longest session we have ever had; are you happy?"

"Yes, I am and here is something for you." Jens handed her a small jewelry box. She looked at him and opened it. Inside was a beautiful diamond engagement ring. "Will you marry me, Laura?" Her eyes welled up and she buried her face alongside his neck. "Well?" Jens took the ring and placed it on her finger.

"That is the most beautiful ring I have ever seen; you must have bought it in America? Of course, I'll marry you; has there ever been any doubt that I love and adore you?"

"Well, you certainly took your time coming up to my room today."

"I was given strict instructions from Anna and they certainly paid off."

Jens went over to the printer and started reading the pages.

"Oh my God!"

"What's the matter?" asked Laura.

"Here, read this." Jens handed Laura the pages he had read; when they were through reading, Jens started reading them again. This time he took his time. When he was finished, he sat on the bed looking at Laura.

"Do you know this person?" she asked.

"Yes and no; I think I have met him when he was at the University for a year, but I'm not sure it's him. I really don't know what to do with this."

"Why don't you wait until his next contact and ask for some clarity; you know it could be one of your friends pulling your chain. You have some strange friends."

"I know, but this is serious stuff if it's true. I'll wait and show it to my dad when they come back; he is pretty smart when it comes to international affairs. Meanwhile, let's talk about us. Do you want to get married now or wait until after the Olympics?"

"My first reaction is let's get married; it sure would make my family happy to have me out of the house. I have been driving them crazy these past 6 months you've been away. However, you and I have worked hard to make the Olympic team; it's a once-in-a-lifetime event. I don't know about you, but our handball team is scheduled to play 9-10 games in various countries on the way to Tokyo. I don't want to take this ring with me and I can't wear it while playing. I would like to leave it in your safe here. What if we get married right after the Olympics?"

"Sounds good; if you change your mind, you know where to find me. You know I'm getting hungry but would like a little appetizer first, how about you?"

"That sounds good, my future husband; anything you desire is here for your taking." It was a good reunion!

Sunday, December 1ˢᵗ at 1:00pm, Jens and Henrik were sitting by the computer in Jens' room. Laura was laying on Jens' bed leafing through one of his trash magazines. The computer lit up as Henrik was sitting there watching it. *The Red Spade* identified himself and asked if Thor was available.

"It's him," said Jens. "He used to call me Thor whenever he and I talked at the University." Thor is here, Henrik typed in. *The Red Spade* says he has less than one minute to transmit. Did you read what I already sent you? Yes, Henrik typed in. I have page #10 ready for your printer. Can we contact you? No, I have 30 additional pages and can't send them all at once; next contact December 3ʳᵈ at 1:00pm.

"He signed off," said Henrik. Page #10 was printing. "This is serious," said Henrik reading the page. "Let's go down and show the 10 pages to your father; is he home?"

"Yes, he should be in his study. "We'll be right back," said Jens giving Laura a kiss. They found Jens' father, Paul, going over some papers at his desk.

"We have something we think you should read," said Jens handing his father the 10 pages. His father adjusted his glasses and started reading. Jens and Henrik sat down in two comfortable chairs in front of his father's desk. Some of the pages he read twice before continuing. When he was through, he looked at Henrik and Jens but didn't say anything for a few minutes. "Do you know the sender?" was his first question.

Jens explained.

"Before I make this call, does anyone else know about this?"

"Laura read the first 9 pages," said Jens.

"Get her down here." Jens went out in the hallway and called up to Laura telling her to come down. Jens brought her into the study and closed the door. "Do you understand what you read in the 9 pages Jens showed you?"

"Of course," said Laura sitting on the arm of Jens' chair.

"I'm going to say this just once; do not tell anyone the contents of these pages; that includes your mother, Jens. This could have worldwide implications if they are real. You say he is sending you thirty additional pages?"

"Yes," said Jens.

"Henrik, have you and Laura had dinner yet?"

"No," said Henrik.

"Call your parents and tell them you are eating here. Laura, go and tell my wife and Anna that there will be two more for dinner." Jens' father punched two digits on his phone. "Erik, are you available this afternoon? Okay, can you come over around 3 o'clock? Thanks, I'll see you then."

"Well, let's get something to eat."

It was a quiet meal. Anna came in and looked at them.

"You know, I usually get some compliments when I fix you your favorite meal. Looking at you, it looks like the Last Supper."

"Laura is pregnant," said Henrik.

"I am not, and when I am you will be the last to know, Henrik." That got the conversation going around the table.

"Thank you, Anna, the food is delicious. I guess we were just hungry which you can tell by our two guests," said Jens, getting an elbow in his ribs from Laura. "Erik is coming over around 3:00pm," said Paul.

"Oh, what is going on?" asked his wife.

"Nothing, he just wants to talk about something we have been working on." Jens' mother looked at her husband but didn't say anything.

After dinner, Jens, his father, Laura, and Henrik retired to the study. Anna knocked on the door and ushered Erik Madsen into the room. Introductions were made and they all took a seat. Jens' father handed Erik the 10 pages which he read twice. He looked around the room. "Do we know this person?"

Jens explained the situation.

"On December 3rd, ask him if he can send the 30 pages before December 10th. Tell him it would be very helpful if he can. I don't have to tell you that this can't be discussed with anyone else. If you do, the circle gets bigger and we lose control. Jens, can you make one copy of this and give the original to your father to place in his safe." Jens went up to his room and made the copy for Erik and gave the originals to his father who placed them in a folder and into his safe.

"If it's okay with you, Paul, I would like to be here on the 3rd of December; I hope I'm not intruding?"

"No, of course not; you are welcome anytime."

"He calls himself *The Red Spade*. Do any of you know if that has some Chinese significance? I know it's not one of their Lunar Years," said Erik. "The University has a large Chinese archive in its Oriental section; they might have something on the meaning."

"Yes, I'll make contact with them; it's odd - Red Spade as in shovel; interesting. When I say do not mention this to anyone, I mean that in the strictest form. I will brief you all when we meet on the 3rd of December. Thank you for bringing this to my attention and I'll see you all then." Erik shook hands with all and Jens' father walked him out to his car.

Jens was looking at Laura and Henrik. "Who is Erik Madsen?" asked Laura. Jens' father walked into the study.

"Erik Madsen and I go way back; he works in the highest echelon of our government here in Oslo, and has been in his job for over thirty years. We have been working together for over twenty years and I consider him my best friend. Can we leave it at that and there is no need to tell anyone about this meeting and the one on the 3rd?" They all agreed on the confidentiality of the meetings.

"Henrik, will you go through Jens' computer and make

sure no one is hacking it or picking up any traffic?"

"We'll go up and go through it now. However, Mr. Skogen, it would not hurt to have the house swept; it would mean getting everyone out of it; maybe go down to your boathouse and roast some sausages; it's supposed to be a nice day tomorrow."

"Good idea, I can get it done tomorrow; take Anna and her husband down there and I'll take my wife on a shopping trip."

The house was swept the next day with nothing being found.

On the 3rd of December, they were all sitting in Jens' room. "You have quite a place here, Jens," said Erik. "It's bigger than the entire house I grew up in, and I had two sisters to contend with, no offense meant, Laura."

"Are you saying you survived two Laura's?" said Henrik. Just then the computer lit up and Henrik went to work. *The Red Spade* informed them he could send 10 pages today and 20 more on the 5th of December at 1:00pm, and further contact to be made in a month; do not try to contact me. The pages started coming.

"Do not misunderstand what I'm about to say, but it would be better if the rest of you do not read these pages or the next 20 he will be sending. You know what it is all about; however, these last pages are extremely sensitive. I will keep you all informed, but right now I have to go over to our American friends at their Embassy. I will see you all on the 5th at 1:00pm. Thank you for coming to me with this." Erik and Paul started to leave.

"No, wait, Jens will you make a copy of these pages for your father's file?" Jens copies the 10 pages. The two men left. Laura was looking at Jens and her brother. "I know what I read, but to me it's not that sensitive, for if it was, how could this so- called friend of yours, Jens, know about it and why would he send it to you?" Having spoken these words, Laura just sat there and looked at Jens and her brother realizing the meaning of what she had just said. "Oh my God," were her next words.

Laura spent the next two nights with Jens. At the breakfast table on the morning of the 5th of December, Anna looked at Laura. "You look tired, Laura; aren't you getting enough sleep?"

"Let me make this absolutely clear. Jens hasn't only grown in height; he has also grown in other places."

"Laura, now you are starting to sound like my wife," said Jens' father laughing. "You and I are going to have a long talk, Laura; after all, Jens has told us that you two are getting married," said his mother.

"Married! How come I'm the last to know?" said Anna. "After all, I consider myself part of this family. This long talk will consist of the three of us."

"What was your family's reaction when you told them about your engagement?" asked Jens' father.

"Well, Jens was very nice; he asked my parents for my hand in marriage; my father got one of his best bottles of champagne and we toasted. My mother asked if she could help me pack and wanted to know how soon I was leaving the house. I have been a thorn in their side these past 6 months that Jens has been gone." Everyone laughed.

Paul announced he had to go into work but would be home at 12:00. "Erik will be here along with Henrik for our 1:00pm session." Jens' mother looked at her husband but didn't say anything. The 1:00pm session was short. *The Red Spade* informed them he would make contact on January 15, 2020 at 1:00pm, and signed off. The printer started and 20 new pages lay there. No one was in a hurry to read them. Jens' father took them and started reading handing Erik the pages he had read. When the two men had read all 20 pages, they sat there and looked at each other and at Laura, Henrik, and Jens.

"You know what this is about?" said Erik. "I'll give you a brief overview. The Chinese have had an accident in one of their biological research laboratories and a virus has spread amongst the people working there, who in turn have infected hundreds of other people unknowingly. To date, over 2500 people have been infected; 325 are dead and the rest are in the hospital or in quarantine. However, the number of infected people keeps growing. The Chinese government is controlling any information about it."

"Where did this accident take place?" asked Jens. "In Shanghai?"

"No, in a city called Wuhan; other places in China are also experiencing this virus. China has informed the World Health Organization (WHO) telling them they have a problem with a virus that started in a wet market (where live animals are sold), but that they have it under control. They notified the U.S. also telling them the same story. The head of WHO has notified the United Nations (U.N) that there is a problem in China; however, he has assured the U.N. that the Chinese have been very forthcoming about the problem and that it's under control."

"I have given the U.S. embassy here in Oslo everything we have received; they are using their other sources to confirm our information. They are not aware of our contact or of you all here; and it will remain that way. They are extremely grateful for the information and are keeping us informed about any new developments. They, as we know, are not great believers in what China puts out and are concerned about the Chinese version given to the world."

"Do you feel comfortable regarding your contacts at the U.S. Embassy here?" asked Henrik.

"Yes, I have worked with them for years and our relationship regarding intelligence has never been compromised on their part. We, on the other hand, got egg on our face regarding the design of a new propeller we designed for the silent running of submarines some years ago which ended up in Moscow by way of Japan. It was well advertised in our newspapers back in the 90's. I will tell you our government, no matter which party is in power, has had a closer relationship with the U.S. than any other country in the world. I'll leave it at that!"

Chapter 2
Revelation

Meanwhile, in a conference room in the Great Hall of the People, in Beijing, the Politburo Standing Committee was meeting to be briefed on the situation in Wuhan. The President looked at the Minister of Science and asked what had happened.

"We had an accident in our biological and chemical research laboratory in Wuhan about 6 weeks ago. The people working there were unknowingly contaminated; some are hospitalized. They went on with their work and their normal life and some of the people they came in contact with are sick and some have died."

"What is this sickness?" asked the President.

"It's a virus, Mr. President."

"How many people are sick and how many have died?"

"We have about 2500 in the hospitals and 325 have died, most of the infected people are in Wuhan."

"How could so many people get sick in such a short time

and what are we doing about it?" The President was looking
hard at the Minister of Science and at the Minister of Interior.
The Minister of Interior cleared his throat and looked at the
papers in front of him. "Mr. President, we have contacted the
districts where the workers in the laboratories have traveled
and have informed the medical personnel that there is a flu-like
symptom and its signs and to be aware and report any cases to
the Minister of Science."

"Have we notified the U.N.'s WHO (World Health Organization)?"

"No, Mr. President, we have not."

"Notify the head of WHO and tell him we have a sickness
which started at one of our wet markets in Wuhan (live animals)
but we have it under control and will keep him informed. The
WHO is the most corrupt and wasteful department in the
U.N. We have bribed him before and let's do it again. Send
your Deputy to brief him personally and make sure he tells
our agreed upon story. The head of the WHO is in New York
for the next month; send a small contingent along with your
Deputy and make sure these people have been in contact with
infected people; have them go out to restaurants and other
public places in New York. This virus could be beneficial to
us if we do it right. I want a meeting tomorrow and all of you
come up with a plan for your specific areas. One more thing,
put out to all hospitals that we will be the spokesman regarding
this problem. No interviews or leaks. Do not alert our people;
we have a big holiday coming up in February; do not cancel or
restrict people from traveling. That's all, tomorrow be prepared
to brief in detail your specific areas."

The next day there was a nervous atmosphere in the conference room. The President walked in and all stood up. He
told them to take their seats. The Minister of Science started
the briefing.

"Mr. President, we now have 2680 people sick which is an additional 180 from yesterday; 9 more have died for a total of 334. All the new sick people are from Wuhan including the 9 new deaths. My Deputy and a delegation of 6 others are on the way to New York and he has an appointment with the head of WHO upon arrival. I have been working with the minister of the Interior and he will brief you on action to be taken upon your approval."

The Minister of Interior glanced at his notes. "Mr. President, the following action will be taken: the military base outside of Wuhan will be locked down; anyone who has been in Wuhan will be placed in isolation along with anyone they have visited, i.e., family or friends. The hospitalized people will be examined and no visitors; if any had contact with family or friends, they will also be placed in isolation and checked by medical personnel. The people in other districts who have shown signs of this virus will be isolated. All medical personnel have been briefed on this procedure. Army units and National Police will be restricted to barracks and are on alert. After our holiday, I recommend that if the virus does not abate in Wuhan, we isolate that city and any other area declared a Hot Zone. I would strongly advise that our military stay on alert during our holiday. Our esteemed Minister of Defense wants 50% of the military to be able to go home and celebrate."

The President looked at the Minister of Defense. "I agree, let as many soldiers as you think go home to their families and celebrate. It could be a severe morale problem if we kept them in their camps. Make sure that all soldiers who stay in the camps are given the best food and drink but kept in the camps; no fraternizing with the local population. After the holidays, I want a detailed report on the military readiness posture; I will add, a true report, not what you think I want to hear. If any get sick, isolate them and the families or people they have been in contact with."

The Minister of Trade was next.

"Mr. President, we have a delegation from the State of Washington in the U.S., their Governor's representatives, who will be here in 2 days to negotiate certain trade issues."

"How many are there in this group?"

"There is a total of seven. A Mr. John Bergstrom, a friend and advisor to the Governor, is in overall charge of the group. Mr. Bergstrom, along with his brother, are very rich and operate many retirement homes for the elderly. They are also involved in high tech companies. A Mr. Jim Clark is on the Governor's foreign trade commission and will talk about lumber exports and high tech. There is a Miss Van Hallegen and according to my notes, she was born in Holland and graduated from the University in Amsterdam receiving her Master Degree in the U.S. She worked for a high-tech company in Seattle. She left the high-tech company and now works for Boeing, where she has risen rapidly through its ranks. She is a very attractive lady in her early 30's. To sweeten the plane deal, she has been authorized to give us one of their new flight simulators which can handle both 737 and 787 passenger planes. The other four men are tech reps."

"Minister Wu, how long will this trade delegation be here?"

"Two weeks, Mr. President."

"I want you to give them everything they ask for but make them work for it. I don't like the fact that the Governor of Washington went behind the President of the U.S.'s back finding a loop hole in the sanctions placed on us by the U.S. President. I don't like people who are not loyal, as all of you know. I want all of the men entertained after the meetings each day by our special female unit. On their last day, make sure each man is given a special present, the virus. Miss Van Hallegen is a special case. I'm sure she will return here to deliver the simulator. Minister Wu, is your Deputy, Mr. Lee, married?"

"No, Mr. President, he is not. His mother is English; he attended Oxford and is considered a very handsome man, according to my wife."

"I want Mr. Lee to take special care of Miss Van Hallegen including a visit to the Forbidden City and the Emperor's private living quarters. Make sure he offers her the special section where the concubines were prepared for a visit to the emperor's bed chambers, if she desires it. Make sure Mr. Lee has the special passes and means to entertain her on a lavish scale."

"Yes, Mr. President, Miss Van Hallegen will be well taken care of. They will arrive tomorrow and will stay at our distinguished visitor's hotel. They will rest the first day and the second day we will start the negotiations, each section in a separate room."

"Minister Wu, send me a short overview of how things are progressing each day."

"Yes, Mr. President."

"Let us meet tomorrow at the same time."

"Mr. President, I have one more item." It was the Minister of Science.

"We are in short supply of protective medical garments and respirators. Until we can make our own garments, we are converting some of our clothing factories to produce the items. In the meantime, I recommend we purchase them from Europe in countries that we know make these items."

"Yes, contact our Embassies and have them locate the areas that make the equipment but don't tell them about the virus. Send a tech delegation over there to makes sure we get what we want. It would not hurt if some of the delegates have been exposed to the virus. I have a feeling that after the holidays we will need all the protective items we can get."

Chapter 3
Trade Negotiations

The 3rd day of trade talks was coming to an end. Miss Van Hallegen was writing down
some items when Mr. Lee, Mr. Wu's Deputy, came over and sat down in a chair next to her. He waited until she had finished writing and asked how she was doing.

"I'm doing fine, Mr. Lee," she said with a smile. She had noticed Mr. Lee from the 1st day. To say he was good-looking and handsome would be an understatement. She guessed he was Eurasian, definitely one of his parents was European. "Have you seen any of our city or been to any of our restaurants?"

"Yes, the other morning when I went for my run, I spotted a McDonald's restaurant and that evening I went over and had a double cheeseburger with fries and a vanilla shake." Mr. Lee laughed out loud, attracting the attention of his boss, Mr. Wu, who gave him a less than complimentary look. "Well, we also have a Kentucky Fried Chicken place about two blocks away; I would like to call on you and invite you out?" Miss Van Hallegen smiled at him and said she would love some Kentucky Fried Chicken. They both laughed. "Can I call on you say at 6:000pm. I know it sounds early, but I would like to show you some places where tourists and foreigners do not go."

"That would be fine and I'm getting tired of eating in my room to be honest with you."

"I will see you at 6:00 at your hotel and the dress is dress-up; I think you will be surprised."

"Looking forward to it, Mr. Lee."

There was a knock at her hotel room door at precisely 6:00pm. She opened the door and there stood Mr. Lee.

"Would you like to come in?"

"No, thank you; if you are ready, we should go; bring a coat because it's cold outside tonight." Miss Van Hallegen brought her coat and handed it to Mr. Lee who helped her into it. On the elevator going down, he whispered to her that her room had a microphone in it and probably cameras. Miss Van Hallegen had been briefed on this prior to leaving the States, but appeared surprised at Mr. Lee's revelation. He complimented her on her outfit and hoped he had not over-planned the night. A car and driver were waiting for them and upon instruction from Mr. Lee, drove them to an obscure nondescript restaurant. It had a small sign outside in Chinese, and a man in an almost formal attire was standing outside. As Mr. Lee helped Miss Van Hallegen out of the car, the man came to attention and made a small bow to them and opened the door. Miss Van Hallegen literally sucked in her breath. The foyer and what she could see of the restaurant was the most elaborate place she had ever seen. The Maître D' escorted them to their table which was in a raised area where they could see out over the rest of this fabulous place. He then took their coats and a waiter wearing a white short jacket with dark trousers asked what they would like to drink.

"I'll follow your lead, Mr. Lee."

He ordered two vodka martinis straight up-dry with olives.

"How did you know my favorite drink, Mr. Lee, or shouldn't I ask?"

"The Chinese part of me knows everything. In all honesty, we received a brief on all of you supplied by your company, in your case. We like to know your likes or dislikes so that we don't embarrass ourselves."

"What would you like to ask me, Miss Van Hallegen?"

"Well, your slight accent is British, so I assume you have spent some time there?"

"My mother was from England; her father ran a large British Bank in Hong Kong. My father was the Chinese Ambassador or Counselor in Hong Kong. They fell in love and here I am. No sisters or brothers. My father was given permission to retire in England after many yours of service to China. They are still living at my mother's estate in southern England and I might add are still acting like newlyweds."

"A lovely story," said Miss Van Hallegen. Their drinks arrived and Mr. Lee ordered for both of them; they toasted and she commented on how delicious the drink was. "Mr. Lee, please call me Erika; can I ask what your first name is?"

"Why, yes, it's Lawrence, after my maternal grandfather who not only spoiled me, but saw to it that I had the best education at Eaton and Oxford."

"It sounds like he was fond of you and you of him."

"Yes, that's true, but what made everything so favorable was his fondness for my father. My grandfather, as you Americans say, ran in the top circles in England and saw to it that my father was included and became a member of the snobbiest clubs in London. Oh, there were some raised eyebrows, but when they got to know my father, they were won over."

Their meal arrived, minus chop sticks.

"I hope you like what I ordered for you, Erika?"

"Yes, it's delicious; no chop sticks?"

"I can get you some if you like, but I have never seen any-one use them here."

"No, please, I would not only embarrass myself but you also. Do you visit your parents in England or does your work keep you tied down?"

"No, I visit them quite often, but each time I arrive there they are disappointed; no pregnant wife in tow. When are we going to be grandparents, is there something wrong with you? On and on they go. I keep telling them I have to find a woman that I like, not some Chinese social climber, of which we have many."

"Your parents are typical and are like millions of other parents. I was married for a very short time, but each time they visited or I talked to them on the phone, they would say - well, are you or aren't you; we would like a grandchild. So, you see, your parents are parents. I am an only child also." They were eating as they talked.

"Can I order you a cup of tea and a small rice cake?"

"I'll follow you, Mr. Lee, if you have it, I'm game."

"This will be our dessert and the tea will settle our stom-achs." The tea cups had no handles on them and the tea had an unusual taste, but was good. Mr. Lee handed the waiter a card and he was soon back with the card and bill.

"I'm not rushing you, Erika, but I have something to show you before we end this pleasant evening."

"Lead on, Mr. Lee, this restaurant would be enough of a surprise for any American." The Maître D' escorted them out to their car and bowed slightly.

Mr. Lee talked to the driver and about 15 minutes later they pulled up in front of the Forbidden City.

"It looks closed," were Erica's first words as they walked

over from the car. A uniformed officer walked out of the shadows and said something to Mr. Lee. They followed him into the walled city and up numerous stairs, walking through an enormous door where the officer left them. A woman appeared in a period costume and speaking good English asked them to please follow her. Erika took Mr. Lee's arm and smiled at him. They passed through several rooms that were unlike anything Erika had ever seen. They came to a chamber where three young ladies bowed to them.

"The next chamber is where the emperor's concubines were prepared for his bed chamber. If you desire, these ladies will prepare you like his favorite concubine would be prepared. You can dispense with some of the events if it makes you uncomfortable.? "Will I see you later, Mr. Lee?"

"Yes, of course."

"Then lead on" she told the young ladies.

They entered a highly decorated room with three onyx-colored tubs. They undressed her and indicated that she should enter the first tub which was half filled with water. The tub was deeper than it looked and it had a calming effect on her as she laid there. The ladies started washing her with a lotion-type soap. When they decided she was thoroughly clean, they asked her to step out of the tub and lay on a soft cloth-covered table. They did not dry her off. One of the ladies explained that they would now shave her.

"In the old days, the hair on the head would also be shaved, but they would not do that tonight. With your permission, they would shave the rest of her body." Erika said yes, that would be fine. They ran their hands over her body, and where they found hair would shave it off. She was surprised at their dexterity in shaving her pubic area. When they were finished, she was placed in another tub and rinsed off. She was then dried off and placed on a table and given a gentle message which aroused her to the point where she felt wetness between her thighs. She was then placed in the 3rd tub which was warmer than the other two; taken out and then dried off and placed on a table and had lotion rubbed on her entire body. One of the ladies said for her to taste the lotion. It was sweet and tasted delicious. She was helped to her feet and a beautiful embroidered silk robe placed on her, along with a soft pair of slippers. One of the ladies opened a door and she stepped into another room where Mr. Lee was sitting on a bed wearing a black silk robe. They were left alone.

"This is as far as you have to go, Erika, the ladies will dress you."

"Not on your life, Mr. Lee," said Erika letting her robe fall to the floor as she slid onto the bed next to him.

"Are you sure, Erika that you want to proceed?"

"Surer than anything in my life." Nothing like the next hour or so had ever happened to her; she was delirious. She was lying with her head on Mr. Lee's shoulders, her whole body still pulsating.

"Mr. Lee, after this, you will have to marry me. I will tell my father what you have done to me and believe me, he has several shot guns, so there you have it."

Mr. Lee laughed. "I am not responsible regarding my actions when I have the most beautiful woman I have ever seen in my bed, especially one that tastes as good as you."

"I'll bet you say that to all your conquests?"

"No, Erika, I don't."

They spent the rest of the trade talks at his apartment in the evenings. On their last evening together, they were lying in bed talking, having been on a first name basis since the Forbidden City.

"Lawrence, when Mr. Wu retires and is no longer the head of trade talks, will you automatically take over?"

"No, it doesn't work that way here in China. It depends on who is President and if you are in good standing with him. I could be way down the pecking order working as a clerk in some department. Do you automatically move up in America?"

"No, far from it; it depends on who is President or CEO of the company; if you have done a good job, you may be promoted or you stay in the same job."

"There is one other thing we have to talk about, Erika; neither one of us has taken protection this last week and a half and I have deposited a lot of semen in you."

"I know and let me be perfectly clear, Lawrence, if I should be pregnant and you might think I have a cavalier attitude, but it would make me the happiest woman in the world knowing that you are the father; I have never met a man including my short marriage, where I would want to be impregnated by anyone but you. I mean that with all my heart, Lawrence, I adore you and you know it. If I am pregnant, we can talk about it when I bring the simulator over here in two months. I will not demand recognition in any form from you."

"We will talk about it when you come back. It sure would make my parents happy though. Having said that, would you mind very much if I made another deposit in you?"

"You have a way with words, Lawrence; I don't' see how any girl could refuse an offer like that."

When he brought her back to her hotel, he gave her a small present. Open it when you get home and think about me."

"Oh, I will, but you didn't have to give me a present; I have nothing for you."

"You, Erika, have given me yourself without reservation; I'll see you in two months." After he left, she sat down in a comfortable chair and thought about the last week and a half. "Erika, you are finally in love," she said out loud to herself. She opened the small box he had given her. Inside was a small jade "Happy God" figure with a gold chain running through where his ears were. She placed the chain around her neck and the fat little "Happy God" hung on her chest.

Chapter 4
Back to America

Upon their return to Seattle, the trade group sent the Governor a written report on their successful trade negotiations, while a face-to-face meeting would take place in 2 days. Miss Van Hallegen met with the executive heads of Boeing and presented them with contracts worth 17 billion dollars with the stipulation that upon the delivery of the 737 and 787 aircrafts, the Chinese had the option of an additional 15 billion worth of planes at the same unit cost. The board congratulated her and the CEO asked her to be present in China when they delivered the flight simulator; to make sure they sent the best technicians to assemble the simulator before turning it over to the Chinese, and to pick the trainers who would teach the Chinese how to use it. Miss Van Hallegen, of course, said it would be her pleasure.

"The board would like to send you on a well-deserved vacation of your choosing at our expense."

"Mr. Chairman, I appreciate the offer, but could we delay

that vacation until I have delivered the simulator and make sure the Chinese are comfortable with it? It's an expensive inducement for the plane order and with your approval, I would like to work in the simulator section until I learn how it operates and then I will know what I'm talking about when my team and I deliver it."

"Of course." The CEO looked to his left and addressed one of the board members. "George, make sure Miss Van Hallegen has the necessary passes to work in your simulator section."

"Consider it done, Sir. Miss Van Hallegen, when this meeting is over, come with me and I'll personally see to your passes." Miss Van Hallegen nodded her head and departed the meeting.

"There is one more item on my agenda today; I would like to introduce a motion to promote Miss Van Hallegen to a Vice-President status. She is smart and anyone who comes back with not only contracts like this, but with Banking agreements to pay for them (very unusual) and to have everything sewn up within 2 weeks, has my vote." The remainder of the board raised their hands.

"Jim, have your admin section take care of the paperwork. We will announce it upon her return from China and the delivery of the simulator. If there is nothing else, this meeting is adjourned."

Mr. Bergstrom arrived at his home and was greeted by his wife.

"You look tired, John. Was it that tough over there?"

"It wasn't tough physically, but mentally they put us through the wringer negotiating; however, we got everything we asked for. I think we underestimated the Chinese; they are not running around in Mao style suits anymore; they were better dressed than we were and I have a feeling a lot smarter. They were sitting in their plush library having a cocktail.

"Are you hungry? I can fix you something; I sent the maids

home."

"No, thanks, what I need is a shower and I know it's not late, but could we turn in early, I have missed you, Jean?"

"Of course, you get your shower and I'll get the bed ready." It was a good homecoming and they stayed in bed late the next morning.

They were having brunch when the phone rang. Jean answered it. "Hi Bill; yes, he's here." She handed the phone to her husband.

"What's up, Bill?" John listened to his brother. "Have you contacted our insurance company and when did this happen? I see; you make contact with them and have our insurance Rep, Ashcroft, at our main office in the morning at 11:00am. "I'll meet you there; thanks for letting me know."

"Problems?" Jean looked at him.

"You know my brother, if there's a ripple in our company, he gets excited. I'm certainly not going in today; I enjoyed my homecoming too much last night and this morning. Can we just eat and maybe go back to bed and continue what we started this morning?"

"Of course, we can, we haven't used that position before; I enjoyed it. I had the deepest orgasm I have ever had which I'm sure you realized. Was it something you learned in China? Now, don't say anything, John; I know your needs and have never complained if you step out of the circle, just as long as you come home to me. I love you as much now as I did 35 years ago when we got married. I'll go and tell Kate and Jenny to leave our bedroom alone and just clean up our dishes here. I'll meet you upstairs." Jean kissed the top of her husband's head as she headed out to the kitchen.

The next morning after a leisurely breakfast with his wife, Mr. Bergstrom headed to his office at their upscale retirement home. His secretary met him and he shook her hand, holding it longer than normal, looking into her eyes. "It's good to see you, Beverly, you're looking good." She smiled at him and informed him she had the head housekeeper who caused the accident in his office.

"Okay, I'll take it from here; thanks, I'll see you later."

He walked into his office and greeted Mrs. Anderson. He could tell she was nervous.

"Just tell me what happened," he said sitting down at his desk.

"Mr. Bergstrom, I.."

"Call me John, Barbra; God, we have worked together and known each other for over 30 years; we are not exactly strangers."

"Oh, I know, but I feel so bad about this incident. I was vacuuming the stairs, helping out one of the maids who was running behinds, when Mrs. Nelson in Apartment #4 must have come up behind me as I was vacuuming the 4th stairs above the lobby floor; I felt someone touching my shoulder. I turned around and bumped into Mrs. Nelson causing her to fall backwards down the stairs to the lobby floor."

"Did you have the yellow caution sign posted at the bottom of the stairs which tells our guests to use the other stairs when this happened?"

"Yes, the sign was present, but I had the feeling Mrs. Nelson wanted to talk to me."

"You are fine, Barbra, don't mention you thought Mrs. Nelson wanted to talk to you; that has no bearing in this. Mrs. Nelson is in the hospital for observation; she will be fine. Remember, you are in charge of this facility; let the maids do the cleaning."

Mr. Bergstrom got up and came around to where Mrs. Anderson was now standing. He came up to her giving her a hug. "When was your last pay raise, Barbra?"

"I think it was 2 years ago."

"I'll tell the secretary to add $3,000 a month."

"Oh, John, you don't have to do that."

"I know, but my memory goes back a long time. Remember when I wasn't sure if I could make payroll and you offered to go without pay; how you comforted me when I was down?"

"That was then, John, and both of us have moved on." They were both standing holding each other.

"By the way, how are the kids doing? They are grown by now." They both stepped back but holding hands.

"Yes, they are; all three have graduated from the University and have good jobs. John is working for our local Tech Company."

"Your husband is happy in his job?"

Yes, thanks to you, John."

"He doesn't suspect or questioned you about your first child?"

"No, and he never will; he loves and adores all three and so do I." 'Okay, you and I are fine and that's the important thing. You carry on and like I told you before, if you need anything, let me know." Barbra dabbed her eyes and walked out of the office.

His secretary walked in and told him a Mr. Ashcroft and his brother were here to see him. "Before I forget, raise Mrs. Anderson's salary by $3,000 a month."

"Will do." He told his brother and Mr. Ashcroft to come in. "Your brother has briefed me on the incident; you had the caution signs out; we will handle it and will work with Mrs. Nelson's lawyers; consider the incident closed, Mr. Bergstrom. "Was there anything else?"

"No, thank you for coming." All three shook hands; his brother stayed.

"Everything else going okay, Bill?"

"Well, we have had an offer for our vacant apartment; it's full asking price. They are only in their 50's; insisted on leaving a $10,000 check as earnest money; will be back in 2 months; they are skiing in Switzerland."

"Let's sell it."

"I was just thinking about you; you use it once in a while?"

"No, go ahead and sell it when they come back."

"Okay, I need to go over to our Kirksville properties and check on the upgrades we made. I'll see you when I see you."

"Say hello to the family, Bill."

His secretary came in and closed the door.

"Are you tied up or can we meet upstairs?" He sat down in his chair; he had been seeing his secretary for 5 years now; she and her husband had a boy, almost 5 years old. It could be his; she had never said anything. After his homecoming and Jean's loving welcome, he had decided to stop the affair but not abruptly. They would continue through the holidays and then he would tell her. God, Jean gave him as much and more than anyone he had been with. It was time for him to grow up. Jean was the love of his life. He went upstairs; his secretary was in bed with just a sheet over her. She had opened the champagne and he poured. He started taking off his clothes but she came and helped him, making sure her breasts rubbed against his genitals as she went down and took off his socks and underpants.

"My, he looks robust but red; has someone else welcomed you home?" He handed her a glass of champagne and gently touched her glass with his. They downed it in one gulp and made love. Afterwards, as they showered and got dressed, his secretary looked at him.

"You seemed distant when we made love; are you alright?"

"When you fly all the way from China going East, your system gets screwed up; it will take me about a week to get back to normal."

"I hope so," she said smiling at him.

He returned to his office and went through the paperwork his secretary had brought him. The company was doing well; they had upgraded the last of their retirement complexes and the reaction from the occupants was more than favorable. The fact that they had been able to do the upgrades without borrowing from the banks, using their own money, was a plus in his own mind. They were free and clear making a good profit. His brother had wanted to borrow from the bank and invest their money in more stocks. However, to be free of debt overruled that idea. He was tired and told his secretary he was heading home and would be at the Governor's mansion tomorrow and would not be in.

"Well, tomorrow is Friday, so have a good weekend, Mr. Bergstrom."

"Same to you; see you Monday." They were always formal when they were in the office area. He was sure some of the help knew of their affair but he had a loyal staff who were well paid. When he arrived home, his wife's car was not in the garage and he was disappointed. He had looked forward to having a late lunch or early supper with her. He greeted the maids who welcomed him home. He asked about his wife and was told she would be home within the hour. He went in to his library and sat down in one of the lounge chairs and fell asleep. He woke to a soft kiss on his lips. He pulled her on top of him and kissed her.

"You look tired, John, why don't you go up and lay down on the bed and get some rest. I'll have the maids bring up some supper for us in a few hours."

"That sounds good. Where were you?"

"We are going to the Governor's house tomorrow so I bought a new outfit. I'll show it to you later; I think you'll like it."

"I don't care if it's made out of gold, you deserve it."

"Hm! You are changing; is it the good loving you have gotten since you came home?"

"I'm sure that's part of it; I'll go up and lay down."

The team briefed the Governor the next day and he was pleased. Miss Van Hallegen was present at the briefing; but left after saying her boss had work for her. One of the tech reps had come down with the flu and had not been present. John Bergstrom felt tired and was happy when a waiter brought him a drink, hoping it would energize him. As he and Jean were driving home that evening, she looked at him and asked if he was okay."

"I feel like someone has beat me up."

"I guess I have to go a little easier on you; we are not in our 30's anymore."

"No, I'll be alright in the morning. We don't have any plans this weekend, do we?"

"No, just you and me," said Jean smiling.

John Bergstrom was not okay the next day. He was coughing, had the chills, and his temperature was high. Jean called their doctor who came over and examined John. Jean was sitting in a chair watching the doctor examine her husband.

"Jean, can I use your phone? We need to get this boy of yours to the hospital." He called the hospital and had them send an ambulance.

"It doesn't seem too bad but I don't want to take a chance. Has he been himself these last few days since he came home?"

"He seemed fine; we had a very good reunion, but yesterday he said he felt like someone had beat him up."

"Hmm, you have to go easy on him, Jean, he is in his 50's," said the doctor, trying to lighten the mood." You know I saw Jim Clark last night and he had the same symptoms as John;

he is in the hospital. It could be something they picked up in China. Are you feeling alright, Jean?"

"Why yes, I'm feeling fine and scheduled for my annual physical on Monday."

"When you go, tell them about John and the fact that he is in the hospital. I don't want to worry you, Jean, but I placed Jim Clark in quarantine and I'm doing the same with John. I don't want you to visit him until you have heard from me. I'm sure a trade session can be stressful and that could be it; he just needs a little rest."

On Sunday, a health nurse visited Miss Van Hallegen's townhouse and introduced herself. She was asked to come in.

"I hope I'm not intruding, but we may have a problem."

"Before you start, would you like a cup of coffee? "I just brewed a fresh pot and am having a cup."

"That would be great; I need a cup." She took a seat where Miss Van Hallegen had indicated in the living room.

"Cream or sugar?"

"No thanks; straight black."

"Me too," said Miss Van Hallegen, giving the nurse a mug of coffee and sitting down opposite her in a comfortable chair.

"Oh, the name is Erika."

"Thanks, Erika, what I wanted to ask is if you have or had any flu-like symptoms since returning from China?"

"No, why?"

"All of the other trade group members are in the hospital in quarantine."

"Are you sure?"

"I saw them at the Governor's mansion on Friday; no wait, one of the tech reps was not there, he had the flu; what's going on?"

"We don't know; they all complained of being tired, chills, coughing, and high temperatures."

"I feel fine; it took me a few days to get over the jet lag, but I have been going for my morning runs. I've started in a new area at work, so I've been bringing manuals home to study."

"Had you been in contact with the other trade representatives after hours when you were in China?"

"No, just on the plane going over and coming back. The Chinese had a dinner for us on our 2nd day in the country which was also the first day of the trade talks. I work for Boeing and I returned to my room each day and had dinner in my room; being a woman who is trying to sell planes in China, you have to be sharp over there; so, I wrote up my presentations each night. I did have dinner out one night with one of the Chinese trade reps, but it was strictly a hand shake affair. I had the feeling he was trying to get me to lower the price per unit or plane. Other than that, I kept to myself. The Chinese are tough negotiators so you have to be prepared each day."

"What about the rest of your trade delegation; did they go out for drinks or dinner?"

"That, I don't know; we stayed at a luxury hotel; I was the odd man out except for one tech rep from Boeing. The trade reps represented the Governor and had their own agenda. We had a short meeting each day to go over problems, but otherwise we were in separate rooms negotiating. The last day we wrote up our reports to the Governor outlining what had transpired and what we had accomplished; then on Friday we verbalized our report to the Governor. I had work to do, so I excused myself after the meeting with the Governor. It's a technical project I'm working on, so I have to study the manuals. Can I send flowers to the people in the hospital?"

"No, not at this time; the doctors are running tests to determine what exactly they are suffering from. If you get any of the symptoms I have mentioned, will you please go to the hospital?"

"Is there anything else I should know? And yes, I will go to the hospital. Thank you for coming over and informing me." The nurse stood up and Erika let her out. She sat down and finished her coffee. So, the boys had caught something; it was no wonder, the way they had been carrying on with those Chinese girls. She had to admit the girls were lookers, beautiful would be a better description. She had not been exactly celibate herself; she was looking forward to meeting Mr. Lee again.

Jean Bergstrom's annual physical had not shown any flu symptoms and the bloodwork was fine.

"I know your husband is in isolation along with five other men. When he is released from the Hospital, wait a month before you have any sexual activity. He is weak; make sure he eats well." She drove home and went into her husband's library and poured herself a stiff drink. God she loved sex, always had; she knew John had strayed several times in their marriage, however her father had been the same. She thought it must be a male thing; they had never gone a month without sex. Oh well, it's not the end of the world. She and John would talk it over and take it easy until he regained his strength when he was released from the hospital. The phone rang; it was John's brother.

"Let me talk to John."

She informed him John was in the hospital in isolation with five other men from the trade delegation.

"Jesus Christ, I wanted to tell him his secretary, Beverly, died at the hospital this morning; they found she was a diabetic and suffered from some kind of flu."

"Oh, Bill, I'm sorry, I know John thought a lot of her. Keep me informed, will you." Jean hung up. John had been at the office Thursday to take care of a problem. Could he have infected others; was it airborne? She dialed their doctor and his nurse answered. She informed the nurse it was urgent that she talk to the doctor right now.

"Just a minute, Mrs. Bergstrom." The doctor answered and Jean told him about John's secretary; could this flu be airborne transmitted was the question.

"We don't know for sure, but that's a possibility, Jean. How did your physical go today?"

"Fine," said Jean."

"How is John doing?"

"He is actually a lot better, but I can't say the same for his fellow travelers. I sent a nurse over to the woman from Boeing who was part of the team and she is fine. It's strange and we've sent samples of their blood to the Johns Hopkins Laboratories on the east coast, so we're waiting to hear from them."

"Should I alert John's brother and find out who he had contact with at his office on Thursday?"

"No, I'll get Bill on the phone as soon as I hang up; thanks, Jean. I think John will be home in a week or so." The phone clicked off.

Chapter 5
Preparing for Lockdown

It was January and the virus was spreading. The Minister of Science was making his presentation; he had a chart showing the rise in both hospitalizations and deaths. They were now starting to produce their own protective clothing.

"The city of Wuhan is being provisioned in preparation to be locked down after the holiday. The military base outside of Wuhan will be locked down." The Minister of Trade was next.

"Mr. President, our flight simulator will be here next week. Miss Van Hallegen will deliver it along with her team of engineers and instructors to teach our people how it works."

"How long will they be here?"

"Mr. President, their estimate to erect and run problem-solving tests will last 2 to 3 weeks; the instructor phases another 2 weeks; they will stay until our people are comfortable with it."

"Where will this simulator be set up?"

"Mr. President, the Minister of Aviation has designated one of his new buildings at the civil aviation school outside of Beijing."

"Will Mr. Lee be available to take care of Miss Van Hallegen?"

"Mr. President, that's all taken care of."

"I want an appropriate present given to Miss Van Hallegen as a form of thank you for she has or is delivering what she promised without delay. She is the type of person we want to keep in touch with if we should need something in a hurry. There are not many people we can depend on, so make sure the present is something authentically Chinese."

"Yes, Mr. President."

The Minister of Interior looked through his notes.

"Mr. President, we may have a problem regarding the virus. Our counter intelligence have received word that someone with Government information is transmitting our close hold information regarding the total number of virus cases to foreign agents to include the U.S. This person or persons is sending information regarding our meetings to include our initial buying of protective clothing in Europe. Our special unit in Shanghai, who have successfully hacked into foreign electronics, have been monitoring these electronic devices and alerted our counter intelligence. However, as of 2 days ago, they have been blocked from monitoring these foreign countries; but of course, we are trying to gain access to them again."

"How can anyone outside of you sitting here gain knowledge of what transpires in this room? If anyone here is talking to impress other department ministers, you know the penalty. Minister of Interior, when was the last time your people checked this room for microphones or bugs as you call them?"

"Mr. President, the last check was before this virus started. I'll have this room and adjoining rooms swept as soon as this meeting is over."

"Anything we discuss in here stays here; no talks in your

homes. Minister of Interior, I want our homes checked also; that includes mine. Do we all understand each other?" Everyone nodded their heads.

"I want the section in Shanghai checked and also our counter intel section. Let's meet tomorrow; I want a report on my desk. Minister of Science, what are our labs doing to come up with an antidote for this virus? I want a briefing tomorrow on our progress; this virus is getting out of control."

"Mr. President, we have an antidote that will take care of the virus; it was included in the notes I gave your secretary yesterday. We are working on mass producing the antidote or vaccine. We should be able to distribute it within 3 months."

"That sounds good; when you have reached 500 million doses, let me know; do not piecemeal it out. The virus is in the U.S. and I want a major pandemic, especially there. It should cripple their economy and hasten our country's economic standing overtaking the U.S. in the next 10 years. Minister of Defense, keep in contact with your Soviet counterpart and see if we can't schedule another joint military training exercise in the near future. The U.S. is watching us closely and any military maneuvers with the Soviets will put more pressure on them. Minister of Trade, I'm looking forward to seeing our new simulator in action. Meeting tomorrow at the same time."

Erika's team worked hard on the simulator and the hours were long. They took a few days off during the holidays; however, by the 2nd week in January, they were ready. The engineers were outstanding. The instructors, of which there were three, were ready and a manual in Chinese was being printed and would be sent to them in China. The Chinese who would be instructing all spoke English, but Miss Van Hallegen had insisted on a Chinese version.

They departed on the 14th of January. The simulator would arrive one day after their arrival in China by a cargo plane. As they were going through Customs, Miss Van Hallegen spotted Mr. Lee who was coming towards her. He said something to the Custom's official who stamped her passport. Mr. Lee took her arm and steered her to the luggage section where she pointed out her suitcases. Mr. Lee said something to a man in a driver's uniform who picked up her luggage and followed them out to a car.

"What about my team members?"

"There are men waiting for them with two large vans which will take them to their hotel near the Civilian Aviation School where the simulator will be assembled."

"Where are we going?"

"We are going near there but to a different hotel," he said with a smile. These were the first words they had spoken. Sitting in the back seat of the car, Mr. Lee took her hand and held it. "I have missed you, Erika."

She leaned against him but didn't say anything.

At the hotel, the valet took her luggage and they followed him up to her room. It was spacious consisting of several rooms. When they were alone, Lawrence took her in his arms and kissed her softly on her lips. She placed her head on his shoulder and just held him. They were both still in their overcoats.

"I have an adjoining room. Your team has your phone number here. Are you hungry? What would you like to do?"

"I want to take a shower and when I come out of the bathroom, I expect you to be laying in the bed naked."

"Miss Van Hallegen! Here in China, we don't talk like that."

"Well, in Holland, England and in the U.S. we do, so get used to it."

"Yes, mam, will there be anything else?"

"I'll let you know when I get in bed."

It was a great reunion. They were lying in bed with her head on his shoulder.

"Are you or aren't you?"

"I'll know for sure in 2 weeks, but I missed my period and am usually regular."

"I know you have just gotten here and I don't want to rush you, but Erika, will you be my wife? You don't have to answer right away, take your time; your answer within the next 30 seconds will be fine." Erika laughed. "You are wearing the "Happy God" so that means you must like me a little?"

"Lawrence, I like you very much; in fact, to be honest, I love you more than I thought could be possible. Have you thought about the future and where we will live; won't it be difficult for you in the Chinese Government to marry a foreigner?"

"I talked to my boss, Minister Wu, and he was not surprised; he told me the President had instructed him to give you a very nice present when you depart China. The President is impressed with you because you are delivering the flight simulator ahead of the agreed upon schedule and that's unusual. Minister Wu said when he was told to give you a very nice present, he didn't think it would be his Deputy; he was actually chuckling when he said that and it's unusual for him to even smile. I don't think it will be a problem; a lot of things are changing in China. Now the answer, please, or I will not give you any more semen."

"Well, since you put it that way, what choice do I have. Yes, I will become your wife, pregnant or not pregnant."

Lawrence got out of bed, went to the closet where his overcoat was hanging, got a small jewelry case out, and brought it back to the bed. He opened it and took out a diamond engagement ring and placed it on her right ring finger.

"My God, Lawrence, that's the biggest diamond I have ever seen."

"It was my maternal grandmother's engagement ring. My grandfather told me to take my time and make sure I gave it to someone special." Tears were streaming down Erika's cheeks. "I love you, Lawrence, and always will. Can I please have some more semen?"

The weeks were flying by. The simulator was up and running, and the Chinese instructors were getting used to it. One day when Erika was checking a valve under the main simulator floor outside the cabin, someone tapped her on the shoulder. She had been bending over and was about to say something when the tap was there again. She stood up with a clipboard holding some manual pages on it; there stood Lawrence with a group of men in dark overcoats and hats.

"Miss Van Hallegen, I would like you to meet the President of China," who stretched his hand out and greeted her. Erika was flustered. She bowed her head and retrieved her hand from the President.

"So, you are the one that's not only selling us many planes, but also stealing my trade negotiator. I don't think that was part of our contract?"

"Mr. President, if you look at the very small print on the last page of the contact, you will see I included Mr. Lee." Everyone laughed.

"Can I see what you have brought us?"

"Yes, please Mr. President, one of your instructors is in the pilot seat and you can sit in the other seat; please go in and he will explain how it works."

The President entered the cabin and closed the door. Erika turned to Lawrence and smiled. "There's room for two more people but I think the President will get more out it if he's alone with the instructor." Lawrence turned and told the others what Erika had said and they all smiled nodding their heads. Minister Wu came up to them and shook his head. "You have lived up to your promise, Miss Van Hallegen, but to take my Deputy is going too far. However, he is very smart not only in trade negotiations, but also in choosing his future wife; you will always be welcome in China in whatever capacity the future holds.

"Thank you, Minister Wu, it has been a pleasure getting to know you and I hope we can work together in the future."

"So do I, Miss Van Hallegen, so do I." After about 20 minutes, the President came out of the simulator with a big smile on his face; coming down the stairs, he looked at Erika. "It's like being in a real cockpit of a plane, flying and landing but never leaving the ground. It will save a lot of time and money training our pilots. Minister Wu, you and Miss Van Hallegen write up a contract for two more of these and we will pay; but make sure there is no small print, I can't afford to lose another trade negotiator."

The President signaled for the members of his group to head back to their cars.

"Thank you, Miss Van Hallegen, the simulator is very impressive; thank your people at Boeing; I'm looking forward to a good and long relationship."

Chapter 6
Beginning of the Pandemic

There was a big party at the Skogen house New Year's Day Jan 1, 2020. Erik Madsen and his wife were present. After a sit-down dinner consisting of many toasts, Erik Madsen asked Jens' father if they could have a short meeting in his study and to include Jens, Laura, and Henrik. As they were sitting in the study, Erik brought them up-to-date on the messages they had received from *The Red Spade*.

"There has been an outbreak of a flu-like symptom in northern Italy; it has been diagnosed as a virus. There had been a Chinese delegation there in the first week of December buying protective medical clothing and respirators. A trade delegation representing the Governor of the state of Washington in the U.S. had returned from China and six of the members had been hospitalized after infecting relatives and members of a retirement home outside of Seattle; resulting in several deaths. Numerous cases have also shown up in Japan and New York and isolation of the cases in the hospitals have become the norm. I have a feeling that this is going to be a lot bigger than any of us here thought; in fact, a world-wide pandemic is a distinct possibility. It will be interesting to hear from *The Red Spade* on the 15th."

"Is there a particular group that's more susceptible to this virus, say old or young?" asked Jens' father.

"The ones that have died are either elderly or have some other medical issue, say diabetes or heart problems. I have not heard of young people being infected or showing symptoms of this virus. I didn't mean to put a damper on the festivities today, but I was updated right prior to coming over here so I thought I should let you know."

"What are the Americans' take on this since they have had cases and deaths?" asked Jens.

"Their medical people and Johns Hopkins laboratories are treating this as a serious problem. It seems the Governor of Washington went behind the U.S. President's back in sending this trade delegation to China and now the majority of cases are in his state. To this date, this virus is not well publicized in the U.S.; frankly, they don't know what they or any other country is dealing with. That's all I know; let's go and join the others."

"Yes, by all means," said Jens' father.

On January 15th at 1:00pm, they were gathered upstairs in Jens' room. The computer lit up and *The Red Spade* said he had 40 pages but could only send 10 today; next contact January 21st; he then signed off. The pages started coming. Erik started reading the pages and when finished with #10, he looked at the group.

"There are now over 100,000 cases in China. Wuhan will be locked down; the virus is spreading to other major cities. The Government is not notifying the rest of the country about the virus. Japan's cases are rising. We know from news media that northern Italy cases are growing at an alarming rate. A Chinese trade delegation which was there some weeks ago buying protective medical clothing must have spread the virus; for within days, people were complaining of flu-like symptoms and were admitted to the local hospitals; some have died. In the U.S., a retirement complex on the outskirts of Seattle, Washington, is being hard hit, as well as, the state of New York with the epicenter in New York City, where the hospitals are getting a lot of new patients. Other places in the U.S. are also experiencing outbreaks, but on a smaller scale. Here in Europe, the E.U. countries are trying to determine what this sickness is. So far, aside from Italy, cases have been reported in France and Germany; they are trying to come up with a protective plan. I'm sure we're going to hear a lot more in the coming days."

Erik handed the 10 pages to Jens who made copies of them.

"I will see you on the 21st. Oh, my friends at the Embassy asked me where we are getting our info from. I told them it was a 3rd party, but we have not verified its authenticity yet. So, I'm going to leave it at that." When Erik and Jens' father had left, Henrik looked at this sister. "Have you told Jens yet?"

"No, I received a letter from the University; I'm supposed to start my internship at the Riks Hospital here in Oslo on February 3rd. I'm surprised they didn't send me up to the Russian border; I've been such a pain to my professors at the medical school while you were gone."

"I'm surprised they didn't admit you to the psychiatric ward; you have been a pain in the ass to everyone. I know one thing, if I break my leg or any bone, I'm sure not going to any orthopedic hospital clinic where you are working; if you pass your internship, which I doubt you will."

"Oh, Henrik! I will take such good care of you; I'll even see if I can't make that little thing between your legs bigger. I know it would make Kirsten happy. That poor girl probably

58

has never had an orgasm."

"I'll see you two on the 21ˢᵗ." Henrik departed.

"You're a little rough on him, aren't you?"

"No, he knows I'm kidding; we used to take baths together in our tub until we were eight or nine, and I saw him and Kirsten in his room through my peep hole. He is well endowed."

"So, you are starting your internship; those are long hours."

"I know, but you will be working for your father; I'm surprised you haven't started already?"

"I know, but I'm getting my feet wet with this intel from Shanghai. I'll be working mostly with Erik Madsen. My clearance came through, after a year and a half; don't mention this to anyone, not ever your brother; although I have a feeling he knows; he has been working with my father and Erik. Please not a word to anyone."

"Does your mother know that your father is involved with Erik's organization?"

"She's known for the last 20 years but never questions him, at least not in front of me. She knows what I'll be doing."

"I'm getting a funny feeling that there won't be any Olympic games in Japan this year; Jens, what's your gut feeling?"

"I agree with you, Laura, and I think we should get married sooner than later. I talked to my parents about it. They will give us the house my mother inherited when her parents died 2 years ago."

"Oh my God, Jens, that's a beautiful place on the outskirts of the city. I can ride my bike to the hospital. There's a lot of land that you have to cut the grass on."

"There is an almost-new small tractor with grass cutting capability in the garage, so you better do your part."

"Oh, I will; I never thought I would ever live out there. I know both of us live in nice areas, but out there everything is open to us: cross country skiing, hiking, you name it. We are lucky, Jens."

"Let's get married; a small wedding; you work it out with our parents. I'm staying out of it."

"Come over here, Jens, I have something for you that I know you like to get into."

The wedding, which was supposed to be small, turned out larger than planned. Laura's parents gave them a week's skiing trip to Davos, Switzerland. They took off the day after the wedding. It was beautiful down there; the snow was excellent and they befriended other couples from Austria and Italy. There was no talk of the virus; all conversation was on a positive note. The common language was English, which everyone spoke to a varying degree. Upon their return to Norway, the taxi took them to their new home. Someone had cleared their long driveway of snow. They entered the house and it was warm.

"I think we have had company," said Jens, looking around. "I'm going to put our skis in the garage; I'll be right back." Coming back into the house, Laura greeted him with a bottle of champagne and two glasses.

"There was a note on the kitchen counter welcoming Mr. & Mrs. Skogen home; the beds are made, fresh flowers in the living room, and food in the refrigerator. Those wonderful people; we are truly lucky, Jens."

"Yes, we are, especially me," said Jens giving his new bride a soft kiss. There was another note on their bed stand telling Laura to come to the hospital on the 4th of February, instead of the 3rd. "That means we will have tomorrow off and we can open our wedding gifts; things are working out," said Laura, placing her arms around Jens' neck giving him a kiss.

Waking up the next morning, Jens heard Laura coughing in the bathroom. He walked in and found Laura leaning over her sink coughing.

"Are you alright?"

"I don't know, I didn't get much sleep last night and I feel so tired."

"Get in a pair of warm pajamas and put a robe and warm slippers on and I'll fix you a strong cup of coffee with toast. You are a married woman now so you can't parade around naked."

"Are you saying you are tired of seeing me naked?"

"No, I'll never get tired of that, but you need to keep warm; remember you are almost a doctor."

"I'll do what you say, husband."

"I'll bring the coffee into the living room; lay on the couch and get comfortable." When Jens brought the tray of coffee and toast into the living room, Laura was fast asleep. Jens took the tray back to the kitchen then placed a blanket over her. He went back to the bathroom and did his toiletry and got dressed.

Laura slept until noon.

"How are you feeling?"

"I'm better."

"I have soup on the stove, so when you feel like it, I'll bring you some. I talked to our parents and thanked them for getting the house ready. Your dad plowed our driveway with our tactor, so it sounds like it was a joint effort. I told both parents you were still sleeping and was told by my father to go easy on you." Laura smiled. "I'm ready for some soup, Mr. Skogen." Laura came into the kitchen, sat down at the table, and started eating. "Our first meal in our house and you had to fix it. What a lazy wife you have."

"I'm sure it won't be the last meal I fix considering your future schedule at the hospital; remember, marriage is a shared union."

Laura drove herself into work the next morning after telling her doctor in charge that she thought she was coming down with something and that she was very tired. He had assured her that she would be fine. Jens had gotten mad and wanted to call the doctor; however, Laura assured him she would come home if she didn't feel well. She made the rounds with the doctors and other interns. It was 2:00 pm and they had covered most of the wards. Laura was weak and was glad when they had a break. She was sitting in the break room with the other interns and had the chills. A few minutes later, she was burning up. One of the interns left the room and came back with a doctor. They took her into an examination room and took her vitals. The doctor got on the phone and called the doctor in charge informing him they had a serious case, and wanted to admit Laura. He was informed that he knew she was not feeling good, but he thought she would get better. The doctor who examined Laura told the doctor in charge he thought they had a case of the virus and was putting her in isolation.

The hospital went into an emergency mode. Laura was placed in isolation in an oxygen tent. Jens was notified and drove down to the hospital, but was not allowed to see his wife except through a window. He was asked where they had been the last week, and he told them. He also relayed that Laura had called and asked them if she could stay home today because she was sick, but they, the doctor in charge of the interns, knew better and told her to come in. Norway had gotten their first case of the virus, but within days some of the other interns and patients they had visited also got sick. Jens drove home to his parents' house but did not hug them; he kept his distance telling them about Laura; they were in shock. He called her parents and told them what was going on. They arrived, along with Henrik. He informed them Laura was not doing well.

"I guess we picked it up in Switzerland. The doctors checked me but I felt okay. I really don't think they know what to look for. Laura had the chills and then was running a temperature; overall she said she felt weak; and that in itself is not Laura. She skied the toughest runs down in Davos and was in good spirits and shape until our first night home. We both appreciate all the things you did to make our house comfortable and welcoming. Laura's comment when we saw the house was that we were truly lucky to have parents like you. I know I'm doing a lot of talking, but to be honest, I'm scared; I'm going back to the hospital."

"You are not going anywhere until you have eaten. I made enough for everyone, so sit down in the dining room," said Anna with her hands on her hips.

"We better do what she says," said Jens' father; everyone took a seat and started eating. Jens told the family he would keep them informed about Laura's condition.

"Before you go, Jens, I want to talk to you in my study; let's go in and get it over with. Jens closed the door; Henrik had also come in.

"We received a message from *The Red Spade* on the 21st; China is experiencing over 200,000 cases with a total of 52,000 deaths. The Government has reported 90,000 cases and 22,000 deaths to the WHO, and that they have it under control. Their cases are declining and 95% of the hospitalized are returning home and in good health. We used your computer upstairs in your room and will continue to use it. I don't know if you looked around your new house, but we, Henrik and I, set up an office in one of the rooms with a new computer, printer, and fax machine. It's the latest technology available, courtesy of our government. Henrik will give you the password."

"I haven't had the time to check the house out yet, and thanks."

"Erik felt it was better to leave your system here and we can keep in contact with *The Red Spade* from here. You, Henrik, and I will get together next week and will outline yours and Henrik's duties. Henrik, by the way, still works for me with the factories as his cover. You will work with Erik; he will let us know what day or date our meeting will be held here in your old room. That's all I have."

"If you don't' mind, Jens, I would like to come home with you now to go over your new equipment; it won't take long. *The Red Spade's* next contact is February 15, 2020, at 1:00pm. He will send what he has at that time. I have a feeling he's under pressure from someone.

Jens spent the next week visiting the hospital each day. On the 12th day, a doctor informed him Laura could go home the next day. It was nothing they had done for her other than keep her comfortable and for her not to have company other than Jens. Jens informed the families about the good news and the restrictions. Anna, Jens' mother, and Laura's mother came over that same evening with two car loads of food they had prepared the last few days and frozen.

"All you have to do, Jens, is heat it up in the microwave and serve it. All the meals are labeled," said Anna as she stacked the meals in the freezer chest in the pantry. "We have been working on this the last 2½ days; there is enough meals and some special items to last you for 4 weeks. When you run low, let us know. One more thing before we go; leave Laura alone and let her rest; she will let you know when she is ready for you," said Anna, hitting Jens on the shoulder.

Jens thanked them for the food and told them he would keep them informed and was sure Laura would call them.

It was a good homecoming. Laura was weak but happy to be home. The 3rd day home, Jens came in from the garage and there was Laura dressed in warm outdoor clothes.

"Were do you think are you going?" asked Jens. "It's time to go for a walk in this winter wonderland; just a slow walk around our property."

"Okay, you're the doctor…almost." It was a sunny beautiful day; Laura tried to make a snowball, but the snow was too cold and dry. They walked around the entire property which was about a mile. When they returned home, Jens lit a fire in the fireplace.

"This is so beautiful, Jens; your grandparents must have supervised the construction of every little detail of this house. Can we have a little warm glogg to celebrate my first exercise in 2½ weeks?"

"The only glogg we have left is the bottle which has alcohol in it; should you be drinking?"

"Sure, but just a taste." Jens brought them each a small cup and they toasted. "I feel good, Jens. I needed to get out and also have a little cheer."

"You call our parents and I'll place a meal in the microwave. Oh, and thank Anna also, I'm sure she bossed our mothers into making all these meals."

After another week at home, Laura called her boss at the hospital and said she was ready to start work; her and Jens were back to a normal life.

The contact on February 15th brought some interesting news. There were now nine cities or towns in China locked down; their big holiday was over with. Over 1 million infected and over 100,000 deaths. *The Red Spade* informed them this was the last transmission; the Government was controlling all information on the virus and was aware of a leak to the rest of the world.

The Red Spade signed off.

Back in Beijing, the standing communities were meeting with the President.

"Well, our holiday is over, what is the status of our infections? You have had over a week without meetings, so you should have many things to tell me. Minister of Defense, I received your report on our "Military Readiness" and I must say it's the most comprehensive report I have ever gotten and it's believable. In it you mention that out of all of our military that's tested positive, 94% should be back to duty within a week; that sounds good. I agree we should wait an extra week or so before we start serous training again. Minister of Science, what have you got for me?"

"The charts I have here are by cities and districts that have been locked down and the number of positive cases and deaths. I might add that like the Minister of Defense stated, 93% to 95% of the people who tested positive are back at home or at work. The greatest number of deaths are among the elderly, especially those with underlying health problems. The deaths total over 100,000. The hospitals are able to cope, although crowded. We are also testing our vaccine on a control group; this is basically the antidote from our lab in Wuhan. I feel we should go slow and not advertise to the rest of the world that we have a vaccine. The virus is spreading and the WHO will declare it a pandemic in the coming weeks; most countries are in turmoil but starting to come to grips with the fact that this is serious. Some countries, including the U.S., are downplaying it saying it will be over by this coming spring; they don't want to panic their people. Their laboratories are starting to test people who have shown symptoms; however, I feel it will be late summer or fall before they start having any success. This brings me to another point for your consideration, Mr. President. Should we share our vaccine with them?"

"I will say this only once.... absolutely not. When they come up with a vaccine, we can revisit this question. The meeting is over with for today; we will meet once a week from now on. Minister of Interior and Minister of Trade, please stay." The other ministers departed the room.

"Minister of Trade, what is the status of Mr. Lee and Miss Van Hallegen?"

"Mr. President, they are getting married at the beginning

of March in southern England at Mr. Lee's parents' estate."

"I want his file expunged; both here and in England. He has been a loyal and hardworking trade representative. I like him and Miss Van Hallegen. I want an appropriate sum of money deposited as a thank you for his services. Use the bank in England where we and also Mr. Lee has an account. You, Mr. Wu, come up with an appropriate wedding present to be given by you and your wife at their wedding, as our representatives. Minister of Interior, when I say Mr. Lee's file is to be expunged; I mean expunged; is that understood?"

"Yes, Mr. President."

"I have a feeling Mr. Lee will get a job at Boeing after he has been properly vetted. No strings attached to him whatsoever. I have personally tested him some years ago and he passed with no reservations. Minister Wu, that will be all; keep me informed about their plans."

"Yes, Mr. President, it will be my pleasure."

"Thank you, Minister Wu, now Minister of the Interior. Your people swept this room and our homes; did you find anything?"

"No, Mr. President, not a thing."

Chapter 7
Unforeseen Entanglements

Li Zheng (*The Red Spade*) was sitting at his desk in the Chinese Department of Commerce in Shanghai thinking of what he had done these past months. The fact that he felt no guilt surprised him. The fact that he had not been caught was a great relief, considering the huge military electronic and spy operation going on in the building right next door to his department. He had actually hacked into the huge mainframe computer about a year ago just to see if he could, but had not activated until about 3 months ago when a friend from his University days had told him about the accident in the research lab in the city of Wuhan and kept him updated. His friend's father was a member of the Chinese Politburo Standing Committee. The ironic part was that the head of the Commerce Department had interviewed him for a potential job in Oslo, Norway. At the University in Beijing, he had chosen English as his language which was a prerequisite in high school also, and Norwegian as his second language. His friends at the

University had made fun of his Norwegian choice, telling him how cold and miserable the country was. In his 3rd year at the University, they had sent him to the University in Oslo, Norway, for a year; he had fond memories of his time there. He had met a Jens Skogen there whom he had nicknamed "Thor", the name of a God from the old Norse mythology. Would he get the job in Oslo? He had no idea, especially since he was a junior member at the Commerce Department; however, he was fluent in Norwegian which was a plus.

Mr. Zheng was getting ready to go to the cafeteria in the basement of the building he worked in when the Minister of Commerce walked into his office. The Minister took a chair and indicated for Mr. Zheng to sit down at his desk.

"I have heard some good things about you, Mr. Zheng and I'm sending you to Oslo, Norway, as our Commerce Secretary at our Embassy there. I'll come right to the point. Norway has sunk a gas platform which will produce gas for the next 100 years. As you know, we are converting our industries to clean gas and we would like to get our share of this gas. Norway, as you know, is a stable country and can be counted on to honor its commitments regardless of the commodity. You speak excellent Norwegian and spent a year over there. I would like you to be ready to leave in 2 weeks. The Embassy in Oslo is aware of your arrival and you will be compensated accordingly as Norway is an expensive country to live in. Do you have any questions?"

"Minister Wang, it is a great honor for me to be given this assignment, especially since I am a junior representative in the Commerce Department. I am sure there are more qualified personnel with more experience who would handle this assignment better than me."

"You are correct, Mr. Zheng; however, you are the only one who speaks the language, so we are counting on you to succeed. Prior to your leaving, you will be briefed by our Internal Section who will answer any questions you have. This is a great promotion for you, so you should be happy."

"Mr. Wang, I am very happy and honored that you have this much faith in me. Be assured I will do my best to reassure you that you made the right choice in sending me to Norway. Thank you for having confidence in me."

"Give any projects that you are currently working on to your immediate superior. I want you to report to our Minister of Foreign Affairs in Beijing the day after tomorrow. Your flight leaves tomorrow at 9:00am; the tickets are at our airline counter here in Shanghai. If there is any confusion, here is a pass which will get you to Beijing." The Minister of Commerce stood up and departed.

Mr. Zheng took his seat and leaned back in his chair; was he dreaming or was he going to Norway? He quickly gathered up his projects and walked into his immediate supervisor and deposited the papers on his desk. He did not say anything but walked back into his office, grabbed his briefcase and computer, and walked over to his living facilities to start packing. He had been seeing a girl but she had started to get too demanding and he was not ready to make a commitment. He would leave without calling her. He would stay at his mother's apartment in Beijing; he would call her tonight to let her know he was coming. His father had died of lung cancer last year. His cell phone went off. He answered it cautiously. The voice at the other end informed him a car would pick him up tomorrow morning at 7:45 for the trip to the airport. He thanked the voice at the other end and ended the call. A car to pick him up – that was perfect; he could get used to these little perks. He went out and got something to eat and to celebrate he ordered a beer.

It was a good reunion with his mother. She didn't seem

too disappointed that he was going to Norway.

"I want to tell you something," she said as they sat in her living room. His first thought was that she was sick. She looked at him in a serious manner.

"Are you alright; you're not sick, are you?"

"No, I'm not sick; I'm still in my forties. What I wanted to tell you is that I'm seeing someone."

"That is great; I'm happy for you. Is he treating you good?"

"Yes, he and I went to school together."

"Oh, did my father know about this old friend of yours?"

"No, he was your father's boss at work. His wife died 2 years ago."

"Will I get to meet my new father? Does he have a family?"

"You stop this; yes, he has two daughters."

"How unfortunate for him; I'll bet they're fat and ugly?"

"One is married and the other just graduated from the University; you will get to meet her tomorrow night; we are going out to dinner with her and her father."

"I hope you're not in the match-making mood; you remember what happened the last time you tried it."

"That young lady was charming; I don't understand your generation. It's not just looks, it's what's on the inside; she had a wonderful personality."

"I don't want to go to bed with personality; I want a looker like you; dad was a lucky man."

"Stop this foolish talk now."

"How is my new father in bed?"

"If you weren't so big, I'd put the stick to your bottom. I don't want to hear talk like this anymore; he is a fine man."

"That's good to hear; I always thought my father was too old for you."

"Your father was a wonderful man. I know he has only been gone a year, but I don't want to end up alone and dried up. How long will you be in Norway?"

"I don't know; it could be years; this time I'll have a chance to get to know some of those long-legged blond beautiful girls over there."

"You better remember who you are and behave yourself."

"Oh, I will, but last time I was there I had to study and did not have much time to relax."

The meeting at the Foreign Affairs section lasted over 6 hours. When he left for his mother's apartment, he was drained. He was told to not only get the gas contract, but also to keep his eyes and ears open to anything that might be beneficial to China. He would be briefed in detail by their man at the Embassy in Oslo. However, their man in Oslo was not his boss; that was the Ambassador. Upon his arrival at this mother's apartment, he went into his bedroom and promptly fell asleep. His mother woke him and he was informed he had an hour to get ready. While he laid on his bed, he realized that in his briefing today, the virus had not been brought up. Was he infected? No, they wanted the gas contract; surely they had not infected him. He showered and got dressed.

His mother was dressed and waiting for him. He helped her into her coat and placed a chrysanthemum in the lapel section of her coat which he had purchased on his way home today. "In case my new father forgets to buy you one."

"Thank you, but behave yourself."

"Oh, I will; I called for a taxi so let the driver know where we are going."

"I've been in a taxi before."

"That's good to know. I will pay so the driver won't think that I'm your butterfly boy." His mother smiled at him and patted him on his cheek.

They arrived at the restaurant. As they got out of the taxi, he noticed a man nicely dressed and a young lady waiting outside.

"Good taste, Mother, he looks rich." They walked up to them and introductions were made. The man seemed nice; the girl seemed shy and was tall and attractive. Her father, Mr. Leji, led the way into the restaurant. A Maître D' seated them at a well-placed table and took their coats. A waiter appeared and Mr. Leji ordered a bottle of champagne.

"So, you work for the Minister of Commerce,?" asked Mr. Leji.

"Yes, you could say that, but way down the table of the organization, I'm afraid."

"Well, we all have to start somewhere, but it's where we end up that's important."

"Yes, that's true, and like the Chinese philosopher Lao Tzu said, "The journey of a thousand miles starts with a single step.""

"That was very good, Mr. Zheng, and very appropriate. So, what is it that you do in the Department of Commerce?"

"I'm heading to Oslo, Norway, as the Secretary of Commerce at our Embassy there."

"The Secretary of Commerce in our Embassy? I will tell you, Mr. Zheng, your journey of a thousand miles is at least half completed. Congratulations on your promotion." Mr. Leji held up his glass of champagne which the waiter had just poured and offered a congratulatory toast to the promotion.

"My daughter has just graduated from the University, a Political Science Major."

"I'd like to make a toast congratulating your daughter." They all toasted again.

"I know how hard you have to study and Political Science is a very difficult program to qualify for. Have you picked your area of study? I apologize; of course, you have, it's a requirement in your last year."

"Yes, I picked the Scandinavian Countries, mainly because their language is very similar, as is their form of governments."

"I didn't realize that the Finnish language was similar to the other three countries," said her father. The daughter looked embarrassed but didn't say anything. Mr. Zheng interrupted the pause.

"Most people, me included, always assumed that Finland was a Scandinavian country, but it's not. The three Scandinavian countries speak a Germanic language, whereas Finland's language stems from an area east of Hungary. They are close to the Scandinavian Countries, but are not part of them. The daughter shyly smiled at Mr. Zheng, slightly bowing her head towards him as a thank you gesture for not making her correct her own father.

"Mr. Leji did not seem put out by being corrected, probably because of Mr. Zheng's diplomatic explanation.

The waiter came and they each ordered off the menu. The conversation at the table was light during the meal and flowed easily. Mr. Leji offered Mr. Zheng a beer with his meal, as he ordered one for himself. However, Mr. Zheng politely declined saying the champagne was enough as he was not used to alcohol, and if he took the offer of a beer, he was afraid he would start singing at the table, not only embarrassing himself but others also. They all laughed and his mother confirmed that her son had many good qualities but singing was not one of them. They all laughed again.. They were finished with their meal and Mr. Leji spotted a friend at the other side of the room and asked Mr. Zheng's mother to come with him as it was a mutual friend. The two young people were left alone.

"Parents are difficult sometimes," she said.

"Oh, you must have graduated at the top of your class, as it took me a lot longer than you to verbalize that fact."

"My name is Thuie, and as you can tell, my mother was of European decent; English to be exact. I want to thank you for the way you corrected my father. If I had tried, I would have failed. You might say my father is very Chinese – from the old school."

"I know what you mean; my own father must be related to him because in our house there was only one way – the old ancestral way. I don't want to pry, but have you lined up a job yet? As you can tell, I'm prying."

"No, that's fine," she said with a smile. "I have an interview next week at the Ministry of Foreign Affairs; what the job entails, I have no idea."

"I was there for 6+ hours today getting briefed on my new duties in Norway. When you go there, don't smile because in all the time I spent there with about five different people, no one smiled; they were all stern as if what they briefed me on was the most important information in China. They all needed to attend a charm school; although from what I saw, they would all fail the course."

Ms. Thuie was now laughing out loud; she discreetly placed her cloth napkin up to her mouth trying to gain a semblance of control.

"Please excuse me, I seldom succumb to loud laughter; you have to excuse me, Mr. Zheng."

"It's good to laugh and smile and to be honest, it becomes you. I hope I'm not being too forward as I have just met you."

"No, not at all; I hope our generation will bring more laughter and smiles; we as a people are far too serious as you so aptly explained about our Foreign Affairs section."

"Would it be too presumptuous of me to ask you out in the next few days, if the weather is nice?"

"Mr. Zheng, I would like that very much; you could coach me how to act when I go for my interview. You see, I'm not a stern person."

"Ms. Thuie, are you making fun of me? I hope so, because I like people with a sense of humor."

"What are you two laughing and smiling about?" asked Mr. Leji as they rejoined them at the table.

"I was just telling your daughter about my briefing at the Foreign Affairs section today since she has an interview with them next week."

"Ah yes, those people are so stern and serious, one would think they bore the burden of the world on their shoulders. They must go to a special school to have a frame of mind like that." Both Ms. Thuie and Mr. Zheng smiled at each other.

"Mr. Leji, I know we have just met, but with your permission I'd like to call on your daughter and help prepare her for her interview at the Foreign Affairs section next week. I spent over 6 hours today with them and like you so eloquently stated, they are a special breed over there. I hope I'm not being too presumptive?"

Mr. Leji smiled at Mr. Zheng's mother.

"Yes, if my daughter agrees, I'm sure your help will be very beneficial. What day did you have in mind, Mr. Zheng?"

"At your daughter's convenience; I have the next 2 weeks off before I leave for Norway."

"Your mother and I have been invited to our friend's vacation place; we leave the day after tomorrow and will be gone for 4 days. That should give you plenty of time to instruct my daughter."

"Yes, if we work 8 hrs. a day and your daughter takes good notes, we should be finished by the time you bring my mother home."

His mother started laughing and soon Mr. Leji joined, as well as his daughter.

"Mr. Zheng, the instructions you will be giving, do they include teaching her Norwegian?"

"They might, Mr. Leji; I assure you that if your daughter agrees, I will help her penetrate that bastion of conceded bureaucrats at the Foreign Affairs section." There was laughter and this time other tables took notice.

"We better behave or they will ask us to leave," said Mr. Leji, still laughing. He signaled for the bill and paid. As they walked out of the restaurant, Mr. Leji commented that it had been a long time since he had laughed as much as tonight.

"Ms. Thuie, if you are still willing, it would be a pleasure to call on you?"

"Mr. Zheng, I would very much like for you to call on me the day after tomorrow. Thank you Mr. Leji for a pleasant evening." Two taxis pulled up and he opened the door for his mother and got in on the other side. "Are her legs long enough for you."

"I'll tell you when you come back from your wild 4 days with Mr. Leji; I hope you are using protection; he looked like he was undressing you mentally each time he looked at you." His mother squeezed him hard right above his right knee. "Okay, okay, I'll behave."

"For your information, we are getting married before you leave for Norway."

"Are you saying I'll be sleeping with my stepsister while you and Mr. Leji are having your pre-honeymoon. Isn't there a law against that?"

They arrived at their apartment and sat down in comfortable chairs. "If you promise to behave, I'll tell you something."

"I'll behave."

"Mr. Leji is very impressed with you and said you and his daughter would make a wonderful couple."

"In all seriousness, I really like her; more than any girl I have been out with. She is a beautiful girl and told me her mother was English."

"Mr. Leji recently retired and he has many friends in the Government; I might say high places. Did you ever wonder what our father did for a living – his work? Mr. Leji was his direct boss and the Foreign Affairs section came under them; in other words, your father ran the Foreign Affairs section as a sub-section in his department. If you and Mr. Leji's daughter get along the next few days, he will have her assigned to the Embassy in Norway, married or not. That is what he was talking about to our mutual friends tonight."

"Well, I wasn't planning on getting married, but I could see myself spending my life with Thuie. I'll talk it over with her when I see her; I hope she doesn't think I'm just trying to bed her; although that would certainly be a pleasure. I have to be very diplomatic."

"I have a feeling her father is talking to her as we speak," said his mother.

. "That's all good, but with her looks, she must have had a lot of boyfriends at the University?"

"According to her father, she didn't date much; it was all studying; I have a feeling she is a virgin, so you have to be gentle with her – the first time can be painful, so remember that."

"Was your fist time with my father?"

"Yes, we weren't married yet but he was wonderful explaining everything. My best girlfriend had a bad experience with her husband the first time and she didn't like sex after that; she just put up with it."

"Were you and my father happy in bed?"

"Yes, he was wonderful; I couldn't wait until we were alone, to be honest. Mr. Leji is the same; we are very compatible. I have told you things I never thought I would share with you; however, I know you have been with women so be thoughtful and kind to her."

Mr. Zheng knocked on the door and was let in by Ms. Thuie. She asked him to take a seat in the living room. She sat down opposite him; he could tell she was nervous. Where to start was his first thought.

"Has your father talked to you about us?"

"For about 8 hours," she said with a smile. They both burst out laughing. Okay, the tension was broken.

"Well, my mother has done the same. So, what are your feelings; do you like me or should we just be friends?"

"Mr. Zheng, I like straight talk and I hope you do also. The other evening when we first met, I knew I would like you; and by the time the evening was over, I knew I loved you. I have never said that to a man before. I dated a few times at the University, but I didn't care for the men there."

"I feel the same as you. When I met you the other evening, I saw the most beautiful girl and knew I wanted to see you again; by the time the evening was over, I was in love. Are we crazy?"

"That could very well be it. Two crazy people in love. My father said he took one look at my mother an knew she was going to be his wife. So, you see, it happens. My parents were very much in love and when my mother died, my father was devastated. I was so happy when he told me about your mother and what a wonderful time they have together. They are getting married next week; are you aware of that?"

"Yes, my mother is in love again. We had a long talk last night and she said she never thought she could ever be with another man, but your father is very kind and loving and she is very happy."

"Are you aware that they are sleeping together?"

"Yes, of course. I will admit to you that I have been with other women and some I enjoyed being with, but there was always something lacking."

"I will tell you I am not experience in sex; oh, I know in theory how it works, but no practical application. I'm naïve and don't know what to do; you will have to teach me. Now am I being too forward, do I embarrass you?"

"No, not at all; you said straight talk, so do you think you could be my wife and go to Norway with me?"

"Yes, I could, if you would have me?"

"I guess what I'm about to say is a proposal. Will you marry me, Thuie?"

"Yes, I will, but you have to call me Lee when you and I are together. It was my mother's nickname for me."

"I can do that."

He stood up and so did she and they came together as he kissed her softly on the lips and held her close.

"Is that what I think it is pressing against my stomach?"

"Yes, I'm afraid it is, Lee."

"Well, come with me." She led him into her bedroom and started to undress. Soon she was standing naked in front of him.

"This is what your future wife looks like; do you still love me?"

"Are we going too fast here?"

"No, I have waited for this for years. My mother used to explain to me how wonderful sex could be and to wait for the right person. Here I am waiting to be loved." He quickly undressed and stood in front of her.

"Well, here is what your future husband looks like. Do you still want to marry me?"

"I don't know; will you fit in me; you are very big?"

"Oh, we will fit nicely together." He reached for her and held her close. "Do you have a piece of plastic and old towel or cloth?"

"Yes, I'll get them?"

He told her to place the plastic on the bed sheet and the towel on top of it.

"Ah, you think I will bleed?"

"Yes, you will; lay on top of the towel." He laid down next to her and kissed her again. She returned the kiss and reached for him with her hand. She gently explored his manhood.

"Oh my; he is getting bigger."

He pushed her over on her back and kissed her neck and nuzzled her breasts, running his tongue over her nipples. She started moaning.

"That's my tender spot sticking a little out from my lips. My mother said you should get me wet especially the first time."

"I will, Lee, I promise you." She was now moaning and pushing his face and mouth into her. She started crying out while thrusting her hips upwards; a final thrust and she cried out collapsing on her bed.

She pulled him up to her and kissed him.

"I think I'm ready for you." She spread her legs wider and he slowly entered her. He felt slight resistance as he gently pushed through; she dug her nails into his shoulders. He pressed forward and was in her warm spot. He held himself there looking at her.

"Are you alright or do you want me to stop?"

"No, please keep going into me; it was just a momentary pain, but it's over." He pulled out and told her to get on her elbows and knees. He entered her and increased his motions. She was helping moving her body back to meet him. She started almost shivering crying out; he gave her a final thrust; she cried out and collapsed on the bed laying their sobbing. He was still in her laying on top.

"Please stay in there," she said wiping her face on the pillow.

He slowly deflated out of her and laid on his side of the bed. She turned to him smiling and kissed him.

"I don't know what happened to me; I don't know where I was, but I'm never letting you out of this bed; I love and adore you more than I ever thought I could like anyone." She reached over and took him in her hands, looking at it.

"He has blood on him, are you alright? I'll get a washcloth

and clean him."

"No, stay the way you are; you are still bleeding a little; it will stop soon."

"That is my blood on you; I can't believe that membrane had so much blood; are you happy?"

"Yes, very happy; you and I are going to spend a lot of time in bed."

"Oh, I hope so. I'm on the pill so we don't have to worry about a pregnancy; but when the time comes, I will be proud and happy to be carrying our child."

"I just hope our children will look like you, Lee."

"When will that friend of yours be ready to give me some more of that pleasure."

"In a little while, he will let you know."

"I'm very hairy between my legs; my mother said I got that from her and also my breasts. My sister has hardly any hair and very small breasts. Are you happy with my parts?"

"Yes, you will never hear any complaints from me about any of your parts. How about you, are my parts satisfactory?"

"Oh, yes, it's amazing how my insides adjusted to you; I really didn't think it would fit, but it felt just right. I think I will close my eyes a little; I'm tired all of a sudden." She fell asleep with her head on his shoulder. He laid there before he dozed off and thought how lucky he was.

His mother came back from her trip and was in a good mood. She informed him she was getting married in 2 days. Marriage meant going to the city hall to register and paying a small fee. He informed her he was also getting married to Thuie in 3 days.

"How did your meeting with her go and did you two spend some time together?"

"Yes, we spent 4 days together, day and night."

"So, you two are compatible and she is happy?"

"Oh, yes, she is happy and so am I."

"I know her father will be happy to hear that. We talked a lot about you two these last 4 days. I hope you were kind to her; it's not easy the first time."

The two weddings were celebrated when the daughter and son got married. Thuie's sister and husband were at the dinner along with close friends. Thuie's interview at the Foreign Affairs office the day after went fine and she was given a job at the Embassy in Oslo, Norway. She would leave with her husband at the end of the week.

Chapter 8
Oslo, Norway

The flight was long with a stop in Amsterdam and then onto Oslo, Norway. There were representatives from the Embassy to meet them and take them to their apartment in Oslo, close to the Chinese Embassy. The apartment was furnished with beds made and food in the refrigerator. They had 3 days before they had to report for work.

They woke up on their first morning in Oslo, made love, and Lee asked if she could stay in bed; it must be the time difference or jet lag as they call it.

"You stay in bed and I will shower and do a few things. If I'm gone when you wake, I will be back within 2 hours."

"Okay, my husband, you do what you have to do; I love you." After showering and getting dressed, he left the apartment and headed for the University. At the library there, he used one of their computers and left a message for Thor saying he was in Oslo with his wife, and would be working at the Chinese Embassy starting in 2 days. He would stay at the

University library for another hour, hoping to hear from him. He had waited about 45 minutes when someone touched his shoulder. He stood up and there was Thor (Jens). Jens held out his hand and Mr. Zheng shook it. They sat down at the table. Jens thanked him for the information he had sent and stated that the virus had now shown up in Norway.

"What name should I call you?" asked Jens.

"Call me Li, it sounds better and easier than Mr. Zheng."

"You are now married; when did this happen?"

"I met a girl and it was love at first sight and we were married after knowing each other for a little over a week; 3 days before we left to come here. She will also work at our Embassy."

"I got married after growing up with this girl and knowing her for over 10 years. We are slower here in Norway."

"I know I just arrived in Norway, but we need to sit down and talk about some things. You must have contact with some Intel people?"

"Yes, you are right; I know some people. How about this weekend; you and your wife are invited to my house for the weekend and we can talk."

"That sounds good, but I don't want to impose. My wife speaks good English but only swear words in Norwegian." They both laughed.

"That's all she needs here, she will get along fine," said Jens.

"There is one thing I would like to ask you; the Embassy gave us a very nice apartment, but I have a feeling it's bugged. Is there any way your people can check it out? At least so I know where the bugs are or camera for that matter?" Can you wait a day or two; be careful what you say or do?"

"That sounds good; I will tell you we are on our honeymoon still and my wife has discovered a whole new life and is very enthusiastic about sex."

"I understand, my wife and I are at the same stage; I for

one, hope it never ends."

"Oh, yes, we definitely agree on that," said Li laughing. "Here, I brought you a phone; my number is on it under the name Thor. It's a present and you will never receive a bill for its use. I would not advertise it; use it to contact me or anyone you trust. Call me to confirm this weekend. If you need anything, call me; I mean anything; we are extremely grateful for what you have done. What is your job at the Embassy?"

"My job title is Secretary of Commerce and my first task will be to secure a contract for some of the gas you are pumping out of the North Sea."

"You are the Secretary of Commerce at the Chinese Embassy? You are either very smart or well connected. In Norway, you don't get a title like that until you are an old man, say 35 or 45." They both laughed.

"I got the job because I speak Norwegian, that's it."

"I have to show you more respect, Mr. Secretary."

"Please, Li, I'm still *The Red Spade*.

"Call me to confirm this weekend; until then, enjoy your honeymoon." They stood up and shook hands.

"One more thing, here is a key to my apartment and the address; thank you, Thor."

When Li came back to the apartment, his wife was still asleep. He quickly checked the room, but could not find any cameras. He got undressed and crawled under the covers and started caressing his wife.

Jens drove over to his parents' house. He gave his mother a kiss on the cheek and asked where his father was. She pointed to his den. Jens walked in and found his father and Erik Madsen along with Henrik. He explained to them what had transpired.

"That is good news; I was afraid he had been caught. Secretary of Commerce, that's a big title; and China needs gas; I think I can help there without raising any eyebrows," said Erik.

"Is Laura off this weekend?" asked his father.

"Yes, she's off until Tuesday."

"Let's get Anna to shop for the weekend and help her with the meals. Erik, you and your wife, Henrik, you and Kirsten and my wife and I. How does that sound, Jens?"

"It's perfect; his wife speaks good English so we are okay there. We can excuse ourselves after dinner and retire into my new den and talk business. He says he's still *The Red Spade*."

Jens called Li the next day.

"Tomorrow, take your wife on a sightseeing trip and be gone form 0900 hrs. until 1500 hrs."

"That sounds good; I talked to the Ambassador and told him I had contacted an old friend from my University days here and had been invited to his house for the weekend to discuss gas contracts. He was very happy and told me to start work along with my wife the Tuesday after our meeting. If I get a line on the gas contract, he will give me a Mercedes; it's 2 yrs. old but in very good condition. I didn't realize he was under so much pressure to get the gas."

"That sounds good; I will pick you up Saturday morning at 11:00am; do you think you'll be done with your honeymoon activities by then?" Li laughed. "It's pushing it, but we'll be ready. Thank you, Thor, we are looking forward to this weekend."

"So are we; casual dress; we are ordinary people." Jens hung up.

Li looked at this wife who was lying next to him in bed stroking his thigh and stomach.

"We are going to get bed sores; we need to shower and go out to a restaurant and get some exercise."

"Let's exercise one more time in bed," she said crawling on top of him. "I have a new idea for us to try."

The apartment was swept and it was clean. Jens picked them

up at 11:00am on Saturday morning. To say that Li's wife was a looker was an understatement; stunning was a better word.

"We will drive to my house and you'll get to meet my wife; she is doing her residency at the Hospital and will be a doctor in Orthopedics in 1½ years. She is off until Tuesday, so it works out nice. The four of us will have lunch and then tonight we'll have company and you will get to meet some nice people, including my parents. The thing I want to stress is relax and have a good time. Next week you both start to work and things can get hectic at an Embassy.

"We really appreciate you inviting us over to your house. I know you are recently married and would rather spend your time with your wife, since she is doing her residency. I know she doesn't get many weekends off," said Lee with a serious look on her face.

"No, we are fine."

They were driving up Jens' driveway and reached his house.

"Is this, all of this, your property?" asked Lee looking around.

"Yes, we were lucky, my grandparents on my mother's side left this for us."

"Oh, Li, you are in trouble; after seeing this, our apartment will not do."

"I knew I should not have taken you out of bed." They all laughed out loud. Laura came out to meet them. Introductions were made; Laura took Lee by the arm and steered her for a walk around the house. Jens and Li brought their bags in and Jens took Li to their bedroom and showed him around.

"Our bedroom is in the other wing of the house, so you and your wife can make all the noise you want, and sleep as long as you want in the morning."

"This is very nice, Thor; I expected a small two-bedroom starter house like most newlyweds have."

"Like I said, Laura and I were very lucky." They went out in the living room and there was Lee and Laura talking to Anna. Jens introduced Li to Anna.

"It's good to see two good-looking couples in this house. You two men have been extremely lucky in getting such beautiful women for wives. You better treat them right."

"Thank you, Anna," said Lee. "I like your straight talk; I'm the same."

"You and I are going to get to be good friends," said Anna as she excused herself.

The lunch was great. Lee entertained them with stories of their quick love affair and marriage and what a great teacher Li had been in introducing her to sex. After lunch, Li asked if it would be alright to walk around the property. Jens told them that would be fine and a fence surrounded the property limits. Laura cleared the table and helped Anna in the kitchen preparing the evening meal. John, her husband, would help serve the supper which he had done numerous times at the Skogen's household. Li and his wife came back from their walk describing their adventure. They found it hard to believe that they owned such a huge property and it being so close to Oslo. Jens explained that his great-grandfather had owned a farm here many years ago. His grandparents had sold the farm and had kept this portion of the land and built this house on the property. The house had been upgraded several times, and now it was his and Laura's.

"We are truly lucky," said Jens. Li and his wife excused themselves and said they would take a little nap before this evening's festivities. Laura and Anna came in with Laura carrying a bottle of wine and three glasses.

"We deserve a little toast," said Laura pouring wine.

"They sure are a handsome couple," said Anna. "I didn't realize that the Chinese were that tall; Lee told me that her mother was of English descent, which is noticeable."

The people started to arrive and introductions were made. Li had informed Jens that his wife was not aware of his informing them about the virus. The people in China to-date were only aware that a flu-like symptom was spreading throughout China, even though some cities had been locked down. John, Anna's husband, served them glasses of champagne. Lee stated that she and her husband would nurse their drinks throughout the evening, as they were not used to alcohol, although they did like champagne. Her mother-in-law had warned her that Li's limit was one glass, otherwise he would start singing and that could affect the Chinese and Norwegian relationship in a negative manner. The meal was served and the conversation around the table flowed light and easily, in the English language. Jens and Li made toasts with Jens welcoming Li and his wife to Norway. Li thanked them for the welcoming hospitality. After the meal, the men excused themselves and headed for Jens' new den. An oval table was located in front of his desk with 10 comfortable chairs around it.

Erik Madsen started out by welcoming Li and his wife to Norway.

"We were afraid that something had happened to you after your last transmission. We are grateful to you for all you have done, and will help you all we can in your job at the Embassy. Congratulations on your promotion." The rest of the men chimed in and congratulated him.

"Before we go any further, can I ask you about your computer; have you deleted everything you transmitted?"

"Yes, I have; but even though I wiped the hard drive, I know you can still get information from it. I was planning on buying a new computer over here and getting rid of the one I have. I brought it here; I don't leave it where someone can find it."

"Why don't you go and get it," said Erik. Li left the room and was soon back with his computer.

"Here is a new computer with the latest technology and safe guards in it," said Henrik. "After this meeting, you and I can sit down here and I'll give you a quick lesson on its operation. If it's okay with you, I'll take your old computer unless you have something on it that you want to keep?"

"No, that's fine; I'll give you the password."

"Okay, we know you want to get a gas contract and we can help with that without any problem. I have checked with the people in the government; how soon do you want it?"

"Well, I would like to stretch it out a little so the Ambassador doesn't think I have influence in Norway. I would like to make an initial contact as soon as you think it's feasible and then haggle a little over price and transportation cost. The usual bureaucratic operation."

"I'll set up a meeting for this Monday at 1300 hrs. at our Oil and Gas Administration; I'll send a car to pick you up at your apartment, say at 1230 hours."

"That sounds good, and I appreciate it, believe me."

While the men were discussing business, the ladies were sitting around the dining room table chatting.

"I hope I'm not being too forward, but I need some help," said Lee. "I was introduced to sex 2 weeks ago and I was totally naïve. My future husband at that time was very helpful and as a result, I enjoy sex more than anything in the world."

"We are with you," said Mrs. Madsen. "We all feel the same way; what can we do or advise you on?"

"Well, my husband is very big and as a result, I'm getting sore and tender."

"How often do you have sex or penetration?" asked Laura.

"Well, 3-4 times," said Lee.

"Three to four times a week, that shouldn't be too much?"

91

"No, 3-4 times a day," said Lee. It was quiet around the table for a few moments.

"Come with me," said Laura. "We are going for a short drive; we'll be right back," said Laura. They drove down to the nearest pharmacy and Laura led the way into the store. She went over to a counter and took a large tube of something and paid for it. They were back at the house in 15 minutes and rejoined the other ladies.

"Well, here is your solution, Lee," Laura held up a tube which said Glide on it. "Now don't use too much of it each time," said Jens' mother. "If you do, it just glides in; you do get some pleasure, but you want the full experience so just place a little on the lips of your vagina. "Does he go down and stimulate you with his tongue?"

"Oh yes, I get so much pleasure out of that I don't know where I'm at sometimes."

"Well, put it on your lips or on his head when he is through down there, but experiment until you find the right amount."

"Laura," said Kirsten, "I'm taking your brother on a vacation for about 2 weeks and I'm not telling anyone where we are going. He has been coming over to my house and falls asleep as soon as we get in bed. After hearing Lee's story, the blood is rushing around my body and nobody better call us in the morning because it's going to be one of those weekends." Everyone laughed including Lee. "I better hide this tube in our room; I don't want the men to think I'm sex crazy; maybe I am, is it natural?"

"Oh, yes," the other ladies chimed in.

Lee came back and was all set for tonight. "I want to thank you all for being so understanding and helpful. My mother died a little over two years ago. She used to tell me how wonderful it was to be with a good man and for me to take my time and make sure I got the right one. I met Li one night and 2 days later I had my first experience and 5 days later we got married and here I am amongst wonderful people who understand me. Thank you."

"I think I speak for the rest of the ladies; we have all gone through what you are experiencing now; however, as you get older and have children, intimacy settles down and it's not every day anymore; another type of love settles in; a more enduring and deeper love. Have all the excitement you can handle now; that tube of Glide will help ease the way."

"Anna, what a wonderful statement," said Lee touching Anna's arm.

It was a good weekend and Li and his wife were good company. Jens took them back to their apartment Sunday night.

Monday at 12:30pm, a car picked Li up and took him to the Oil and Gas Headquarters in Oslo. A man came out and held out his hand.

"Secretary Zheng, my name is Larsen."

They shook hands and Larsen took Li up to the 3rd floor and into a room where three other men were. Introductions were made. They all took their seats and Mr. Larsen explained the situation. They spoke the Norwegian language and Li felt comfortable.

"We call this stage of the negotiation the initial phase; no final decision will be made today, but we will continue meeting. It takes time to iron out all the details and I'm sure you have people in China you want to consult with as we progress; however, we here see no obstacles to a good contract." Li spoke and thanked them for this initial meeting and hoped that they would have a long and good working relationship. The meeting lasted 2 hours and a date was set in which to continue negotiations.

Li went from the meeting to the Chinese Embassy and was taken in to meet the Ambassador. He relayed to him what had transpired this weekend and his meeting with the Norwegian Oil and Gas people; also included was info about their next meeting. The Ambassador came around to where Li was now standing and shook his hand while congratulating Li. He then went back to his desk and pressed a button on his phone. The door opened and his secretary came in; the Ambassador gave her instructions to get Minister Zheng an international driver's license and to show him his office. She made a slight bow and escorted Li into his own office. It was larger than he had expected and with a conference table. The secretary told him she would be right back. In about five minutes, she arrived with a man who carried a camera and had some forms in his hand. Li's picture was taken and he filled the forms out. The man departed and soon returned with a small form with Li's picture on it. He explained to Li that he must carry this with him at all times; that he had Embassy status now and his vehicle was waiting downstairs in the garage. He would take Li down and show him the vehicle and answer any questions he had.

The vehicle looked brand new, but the man explained it was 2 years old and had just been serviced by the Mercedes dealership. Li sat behind the steering wheel and looked at the instrument panel. The man showed him a road regulation book on Norwegian signs and laws for Li to study. Normally this vehicle did not need a key to start it, but the Embassy had all their vehicles modified so a key was needed. Li received two keys and instructions on how to use them; pressing a section on the key would open and lock the door; it would also open the trunk. It was a 4-door dark blue vehicle with a gray leather interior. If Li needed to fill it with gas, he had two alternatives: he could buy the gas himself using the high-octane type, or he could bring it into the garage where they were sitting and it would be filled up at no charge. Li thanked the man, closed the door, and drove out of the garage and home to his apartment; there was a parking place for him with a number that corresponded to his apartment.

Chapter 9
A Fly in the Ointment

Secretary Zheng (Li) was sitting in his office going over some contracts, but his mind was not on his work. He kept reflecting on his good fortune; his Commerce section at the Embassy had expanded and he now had three additional people working for him. They had bought a house on the outskirts of Oslo with about 1½ acres of land around it and his wife was delirious with happiness. He had used the money his father-in-law back in China had given him when he and Lee had gotten married. His salary at the Embassy had risen when the gas contracts had been signed, and in consultation with the Ambassador and the Department of Commerce back in China, had convinced the Minister of Trade to buy four gas container ships from a Norwegian Consortium, which in the long run would save China money. So why wasn't he happy? They had paid kontant (cash) for the house and its furniture and they had no bills. They were making good money, and in good-old Chinese custom, placed half of their salary each month in the bank.

He needed to call over to his wife's office and see if she was available for a nice lunch or maybe a trip to their home for a nap. They called it a nap; in reality it was a chance to make love, which broke the day up and always put both of them in a good mood. He pressed his intercom button and heard voices; it was his wife and her boss talking in loud voices. His wife must have left her intercom on forgetting to turn it off. He was about to press his button off when he heard his wife literally chewing her boss out. She told him if he didn't comply with her instructions, she would have him sent back to China in irons (chains) and he knew damn well what would await him there. Her supposed boss was apologizing and informed her he would take care of the situation. He heard a door close and turned off the intercom sitting back in his chair. Had he heard correctly? Yes, it had been his wife Lee instructing her boss. What was going on? Was his wife in charge of the Foreign Affairs section of the Embassy? She had graduated from the University in Beijing majoring in Political Science 4 months ago, prior to them getting married and moving to Norway. It was well known that the Foreign Affair's office in most of China's Embassies ran the intelligence section whose people had covers such as military attaché, industrial advisors, etc. There had to be an explanation for his wife's outburst. In the almost 4 months of marriage, they never had a disagreement; it was almost unheard of. He had mentioned this to Jens once who had admitted that he and Laura, his wife of little over a year, had disagreements which most newly married people had. Jens had attributed Li's bliss to him training his wife right, and could he give Jens some tips on what Li had done right and what he was doing wrong in training his wife. This had all been in jest, but as Li sat there and reflected, Lee had never raised her voice even when he had thought she had a reason. He was confused; he had to talk to someone; that someone would be his best friend and confidant, Jens.

Li left his office telling his secretary he would be back in 2 hours. He went down to the Embassy garage and drove down to the harbor where people kept their private boats. He parked and walked about a block along the seawall to where there were some empty benches. He dialed Jens' number and the call was answered on the 3rd ring.

"Ah, Mr. Secretary, what can your humble servant do for you today?" Li informed him he was sitting on a bench overlooking the area where he used to watch Jens practicing with his rowing teammates, and could he join him right away? "I'll be there in 15 minutes." The phone clicked off.

Jens arrived and sat down next to Li.

"Have you had lunch yet?" asked Jens.

"No, I haven't."

Jens got up and went over to a lunch wagon and bought them two hot dogs with mustard and two small soft drinks.

"Okay, now eat; I know you like hot dogs." Li smiled at him and started eating.

"Now, what is so important that I had to rush down here in the middle of my lunch?"

"Oh, I'm sorry, I just need to talk to someone."

"I'm not serious, Li, I was in a boring meeting and almost fell asleep; I needed to get out of there." Li relayed what had happened and how confused he was.

"Are you sure you heard correctly? It doesn't sound like Lee."

"I know, but I know what I heard and it was Lee and her boss. She was giving him orders. You know what the Foreign Affairs section does at our Embassy, don't you?"

"Yes, every country has a Foreign Affairs section; that's why I was surprised when you first arrived in this country and told me what Lee's job was. Somehow she doesn't fit that role. My guidance to you is to not confront her yet; let it ride awhile."

"I agree with you. Lee is heading to Sweden for 2 days, leaving the day after tomorrow; maybe there is an explanation for this; I don't know?"

"Do you want to come over to the house while she is gone?"

"No, thanks, I promised her I would build some flower boxes and fix the areas up around the house; I'm a good carpenter and have bought the tools and lumber. I'll have it done by the time she gets back."

"Okay, if you need some help, give me a call."

"Thanks, Jens, there is one other thing. Lee and I had been looking at houses before you alerted us to the one we bought. How come that house was so much cheaper than the houses we looked at which had no land around them."

"If I remember right, was it not a case where the couple you bought if from were getting a divorce?"

"That's true, but why such a low price?"

"It wasn't cheap, Li, as I remember; although I haven't been looking at houses so I'm not up-to-date in that area. I will say to ease your mind that there are a lot of people that feel they owe you a lot for what the chance you took."

"Thank you, Jens, I feel I can always count on you, and you on me if it comes to that. I better get back to work. I'll take your advice and not mention anything to Lee."

"Call me if you need me," said Jens getting into his car.

Jens was troubled by what Li had told him. He drove to his parents' house and walked in saying "hello" loudly. Anna appeared and told him his parents were out shopping, for what she didn't know.

"Have you got time to listen to an old lady?"

"Sure, what's up?"

"I don't know where to start, but I feel I have to tell

someone. Lee and I have become good friends and she tells me things. The other day she told me that her and Li have problems. It's not anything overt, it's just that when they are intimate, he seems to be just going through the motions, not at all like him. She says she tried to lighten things up, but he doesn't respond like he used to. I asked if she thinks it's his work and if he's just tired. I told her work pressure can affect a man's reaction in bed. She says he likes his job and has received praises both from the Ambassador and from China. I asked if she thinks there is another woman in the picture, but she doesn't think so."

"Anna, are they still going at it 3-4 times a day?"

"No, they are down to 2-3 times, which worries her also."

"Are you serious, he's not a machine. If Laura and I had sex 3-4 times or 2-3 times a day for months at a time, I would be dead. I can see if you have been apart for weeks, maybe for a few days, but not months, Anna."

"I know, I wanted to ask her what kind of pills Li was on so I could get some for John, but I didn't go there."

"I don't know, Anna, I'm glad you told me; did she say anything else?"

"It's funny you ask, a month or so ago she asked if we were being so nice to her and Li because of the information Li had sent us while he was still in China. I told her I didn't know what she was referring to and I hoped that her and I were still having straight talk like we said we would when we first met." Jens got up and said to Anna not to discuss what she had just said to anyone else. He gave her a kiss on her cheek and left.

Jens called his father and asked him to get Erik and Henrik and meet him at his house; it was very important. About 45 minutes later, the four people were sitting in Jens' den. He told them about the conversations he had with Li and with Anna.

"I'll tell you, when they showed up here in Oslo, married

after knowing each other for less than a week, I told Henrik that it seemed too contrived," said Erik looking at the others.

"She will be in Sweden for 2 days; I'll alert our Embassy there to follow her and see what she's up to."

"Li told me when they first got here that his wife did not know about his messaging to us and he wanted it kept that way. I talked to him about 2 months ago, right after they moved into their house, and we talked about the virus which has now been designated a pandemic by the WHO. He told me he was glad he hadn't told his wife about the information he sent to us because of the job she has at the Embassy. The other thing I find unbelievable is their 3-4 times activities in bed each day that she told the wives about, and has told Anna they are now down to 2-3 times a day. Li has never mentioned anything about their intimacy. He seems in good shape and I don't think he is on any drugs."

"So, do we wait and see and wait until she returns from Sweden?"

"I agree with Jens, there has been several comments made by Lee that's a little far out; if she is what we think she is, she is not a good story teller, especially what she told Anna. She may be trying to draw us out; I don't think she is aware that myself, Jens, and Henrik are involved in your organization, Erik. She is probably wondering what we do, or what Jens and Henrik do for a living. I'm sure she knows about my factories; that's public knowledge. Can we meet, say, every other day when she comes back from Sweden and let's meet in Jens' old room."

"I don't see why not, but let's not meet just to meet, only if there is something new, and I'll bring you up to date on her trip."

There were no meetings. Erik let them know he would be in meetings at the American Embassy the next 3 days and would contact them later.

Jens was working at his office, adjacent to Erik's, on some problems at the border with Russia when Erik walked in and told him to call his father and Henrik and to meet them in Jens' old room. It took an hour for them to get together. Erik explained what had transpired the last 4 days. The Chinese Ambassador to Sweden and his wife had been found dead at the Ambassador's residence in Stockholm. They had dinner the night before with a Chinese man and woman at their residence. According to their maid, it had been a congenial event and their guests had departed at 9:30pm. The maid had never seen this Chinese couple before, but the Ambassador's wife had told the maid the day before that they were having guests the following evening and to tell the cook that the dinner was to be served at 7:00pm. That's all the information that had been told to the Swedish authorities as this was an internal investigation being handled by the Chinese. The fact that they got any information at all was because the Ambassador and his wife had a private home located in the outskirts of Stockholm.

Now, our people at our Embassy in Stockholm had followed Lee and her supposed boss when they arrived at the airport in Stockholm. They stopped for an hour at the Chinese Embassy arriving there at 11:00am and departing at 12:00pm. They drove to a small restaurant on the outskirts of Stockholm, had lunch arriving there at 1:30pm and left the restaurant at 2:45pm. They drove around arriving at the Ambassador's residence at 6:00pm. When they departed the residence at 9:30pm, they drove to the airport and boarded a plane for Oslo. Our people here picked them up on arrival in Oslo and followed them to the Chinese Embassy. Lee stayed at the Embassy for half an hour departing at 12:15 and was driven home arriving at her house at 12:40. So, Lee was gone one day instead of two. According to our friends at the American Embassy, there is turmoil at the Chinese Foreign Affairs and the Counselor Section in Beijing. Initial reports from their Embassy in Stockholm point to poison. The Ambassador and his wife had gone to bed after their dinner. In the morning when the maid came into their bedroom to check on them, they were unresponsive. Lee and her "Boss" got recalled to Beijing and left the next morning on a KLM flight to Amsterdam, changed planes and took KLM to Beijing. Our friend at the U.S. Embassy also informed me that there had been problems at the Chinese Embassy in Stockholm for months. Sweden, as you know, has been a conduit for North Korea, Vietnam and China for years, funneling money to various scientific projects and in the case of North Korea, missiles. However, the Swedish National Bank has come under the EU scrutiny and allegations of impropriety to include money laundering. A large Swedish project in China was canceled by Sweden for unknown reasons; however, it was alleged that the Chinese Embassy had scuttled the project when supposed pak money (bribes) had not been paid to certain Chinese at their Embassy in Stockholm."

"Should I give Li a call to invite him and his wife to our house?"

"Yes, by all means; I don't think he is involved," said Erik. Jens called and Li answered.

"I'm calling to invite you and Lee to a small dinner at our house this weekend; are you free?"

"Jens, let me call you back in about an hour." The phone went dead.

"I have a tray of sandwiches and coffee down here but one of you will have to come down and get it," Anna yelled up to them.

"I love you, Anna," Henrik yelled down to her. "I'm coming down to get it."

Henrik went down and took Anna in his arms and kissed her on the cheek. "Let go of me; I'm not one of those women you can have your way with. I'm going to tell Kirsten how you behave when she is not around."

"She already knows; thanks for the tray of goodies. The others upstairs would let me starve; they get so involved in business. Thanks again."

"I don't mean to come on so strong, you can give me a hug and kiss anytime."

"Ah, so you are one of those women?"

"We heard you down there, you aren't trying to romance Anna, are you? Asked Jens' father.

"If I was a little older and had met her before John, you bet I would – the way she cooks, just look at this tray." They ate every morsel on the tray.

"This hit the spot," said Erik. We should get a call any time," said Jens.

"I wonder how Li likes batching it? I wonder if Lee will be back?"

"The Chinese hold their cards close to their chests; it's hard to tell," said Erik.

The phone rang. "I had to leave the Embassy; too many ears," said Li.

"You sound down; are you alright?"

"Not really; Lee and her boss got called back to Beijing when she came back from Sweden. She caught the virus and is in the hospital not doing so good. All of us at the Embassy got tested, but we are okay. She must have gotten it on the plane. I talked to my mother; they won't let anyone in to see her; she is in isolation. The Ambassador gets an update each day. Her boss did not get infected; it's strange."

"I told you about Laura when she got infected but not me. Lee will be alright. Do you need anything; a good meal?'

"Thank you, I'm fine; the strange part is they won't let me go back to see her; only essential people are allowed into

China now. The U.S., as you know, will not let any Chinese or European flights into their country unless it's essential travel. This has turned into a mess, Jens."

"I know, Li; if you need anything, you better let me know. Do I have your word?"

"Yes, Jens, thank you, I better get back to work." The phone went dead.

Jens had the phone on speaker so all heard the conversation.

"I don't want to sound pessimistic, but Lee is dead or will be in the next few days," said Erik with a somber face. It doesn't take a genius to figure out that she was involved in the Embassy deaths in Sweden. She may have had instructions to do away with them, but she visited the Embassy and then dinner with the Ambassador and his wife, not a good operation."

"If you hear from Li in the couple of days, let us know, Jens."

"If he calls or comes over to my house, should I tell him about his wife's comment to Anna?"

"Hold off on that, I don't think he will be allowed to go back for her funeral so he's going to need a sympathetic ear. We need to come up with a plan based on what he tells you, Jens."

Two days later Jens got a call from Li. Could they meet at the usual place? Jens got there first and watched as Li walked up to him.

"Are you alright, Li?"

"No, I'm not; Lee died last night and she will be buried today. China is experiencing a lot of virus deaths and they are burying them right away. I talked to my mother and Lee's father; they are devastated; the government would not even let them see her body. Lee's father has a lot of friends high up in the Government, but was only informed about her death. I assume she will be cremated, which according to Lee's father, is what the Government is doing now. I am to stay in Norway until this virus settles down. I don't know what to do. I asked the Ambassador why Lee was recalled, but all he received according to him was a notice to send her and her boss back to China immediately; no reason. He did inform me that the Ambassador to Sweden and his wife had died all of a sudden. Their Commerce section is in turmoil for some reason and I might have to go over there for a few weeks, but that's only tentative; he will keep me informed. The Ambassador is having a small get-together the day after tomorrow to honor Lee. That's all I know. I really don't know what to do now. I'll probably sell the house and move into one of the Embassy's apartments; I don't know."

"Li, don't sell the house yet; let all this settle down. I'm like you; I'm devastated; it's easy for me to give advice because I'm not in your shoes. However, in the not-too-distant future, we need to sit down and have a long talk; in the meantime, after the Ambassador's get-together, you are coming over to our house. You can come tonight and stay if you want; you are welcome anytime, Li; our door is always open to you."

"I know, Jens, and I have never had a friend like you. I'll call you in a few days and give my best to Laura; she deserves someone better than you."

"I know that and you know that, but don't you ever tell her, because she will agree with you. Take care, Li, and like I said, come over anytime."

It was 3+ weeks before Jens got a phone call from Li. He told Jens he had been in Sweden getting the Commerce section at the Chinese Embassy straightened out and was now back in Oslo and could they have a meeting at Jens' house with his friends as he had a lot to talk to them about. Jens informed him he would set-up a meeting and would let him know the next day.

"Are you alright, Li? You have had a lot on your plate this

last month and we were starting to worry about you."

"Yes, thanks, Jens, I'm doing okay; Sweden was a mess and kept my mind off other things. I'll await your call." The phone went dead. Jens sat there and thought about the phone call; something was not right and Li sounded anxious. Erik walked into his office and looked at Jens.

"You look like you got bad news, what's going on?"

"I just had a call from Li; he didn't sound right and wants to have a meeting as soon as possible. He had been at the Chinese Embassy in Sweden; there is something going on."

"Interesting, I just got off the phone with your father; he wants to have a meeting tomorrow morning, if possible, at his house. He has set up your old room with a conference table and made it into a meeting room. What if we meet in the morning and get your father's agenda taken care of and then have Li come over say around 11:30 or 12:00. I'll call that catering service and have them set up a cold board at 12:00 hours and have Li join us. They usually put out a nice meal; that way we won't have to bother Anna."

"It sounds good, but you will have to explain to Anna why we are having food brought in instead of letting her fix our meal."

"I know, but we have this contract with them and we pay whether or not we use them."

Jens called Li and told him when and where tomorrow and to not eat lunch. Li's voice sounded strained and said he would be there at 12:00 hrs.

"I don't know," said Jens. "I guess we will find out tomorrow what's on his mind."

Jens told Laura about meeting with Li the next day. She looked at Jens and asked how Li was coping with the loss of Lee.

"I don't know, the last time I met with him he was down and like I told you was thinking about selling their house. I think I talked him out of making any sudden decisions and then he went to Sweden for 3+ weeks; when I talked to him today, he didn't sound right."

"I'm off for the next 2 days and going shopping with Anna and your mother tomorrow; however, as your personal doctor-to-be, I need to check you out this evening as my time has been limited these past two weeks; to make sure your parts are still working. I realized today at the Hospital when I saw an old man lying in bed and he was looking good to me that my needs have not been taken care of." Jens took her arm and led her into the bedroom and started undressing her.

The meeting the next morning brought some good news. The U.S. Navy and Marine Corps had decided to buy the new anti-ship and ship-to-shore missiles built by Jens' father's factories. The missiles had been in use by four NATO countries for the last 2 years and were proving to be reliable and effective. A U.S. missile company, which had for years been working with his father's factories, would help build them in the U.S. The contract which had been signed already was worth over a half a Billion U.S. dollars to his factories. Kudos were heaped on Jens' father. Henrik and one of the engineers would be leaving for Tucson, Arizona, in a month. Meanwhile, Henrik and Kirsten were getting married next week.

"Well, it's about time," said Erik. "Why should you be the only one amongst us who is not saddled with a wife. Welcome to the chain gang, Henrik, I can assure you it's not all bad. All kidding aside, congratulations; Kirsten is a fine young lady."

"The other business we have to discuss is Li. He will be here in an hour. I think it's time to be open with him and let him know what his wife told Anna; he deserves that much from us."

"When I talked to him yesterday, he seemed anxious or hyper; I think we should evaluate what we tell him once he gets here and have lunch and then come up here and determine his frame of mind," said Jens. The others agreed.

The doorbell rang. "I think our friends are here," said Erik getting up. "Should I tell them to set it up in the dining room?"

"That will be fine," said Jens' father. They all got up and went downstairs. Jens showed the caterers where to set up the food; it was a lavish display of culinary effort. Erik signed the bill and the caterers departed. Li walked in as they were leaving and asked if this was his homecoming feast. They all shook his hand and welcomed him back.

"Let's eat while some of these dishes are still warm," said Erik.

"We have missed you, Li," said Jens. "You look tired and look like you could use a good meal." Li agreed and said he was happy to be back among friends. He described the turmoil in Sweden. The Ambassador in Oslo had been authorized to promote him, based on what he had accomplished in Sweden. He had a lot to talk to them about after the meal. The mood around the table was light and Li seemed to have snapped out of his anxious mood.

When they regrouped upstairs and sat around the table, Li made a statement which changed everything.

"I want to tell you that Lee didn't get the virus; she died of a poison along with her supposed boss in a hospital in Beijing. They used the virus as a cover. They had both been in Sweden when the Chinese Ambassador and his wife were poisoned. The person who poisoned them was the cook, who by the way, is part of the Chinese Intelligence Service. Lee and her boss had just been in the wrong place at the wrong time. The cook had told them to fly back to Norway that evening. When Lee got home that night, she was extremely upset and told me she thought she was in trouble, but wouldn't say why, other than they had been used as a cover for a Chinese intelligence operation and would probably be recalled to China. In the morning prior to going to work, she received a telephone call from the Ambassador telling her to go directly to the airport; a car would pick her up, and to pack a suitcase with only essential items. She left the house and I never saw her or heard from her again. When I was in Sweden, a friend of mine from the University days, and by the way the person who gave me all the information I passed onto you, arrived to take over the Commerce section at the Embassy. He informed me what had taken place and that the Chinese were using the virus to get rid of people they found lacking. Li asked if he could talk openly for what he had to say was sensitive. Erik assured him he was safe and anything said would stay in the room.

"I have a conflict," said Li. "The first is that I have been thinking of defecting either to Norway or the U.S. The other solution would be that I continue my job at the Embassy and also continue to inform you about any intelligence I come across regarding China. I was not caught when I sent you the intelligence about the virus, but according to my friend, the counter intelligence in Shanghai suspected me or someone in the Commerce Department of hacking into their network. However, they were not able to prove it to the point where they could accuse me or anyone else because a foreign nation was successful in placing what my friend called a firewall or block on the entire operation in Shanghai; their computers were hacked or wiped clean causing them a lot of work which took them months to reconstruct. I'm not a computer expert so what happened to their system is beyond me. I can give you some information about Russia, which both you and the U.S. will find interesting. Do you have a recorder I can speak into because this information is fresh in my mind?"

"When you are ready, Li, start talking, but do a disclaimer in which you state that you are not under duress and that you voluntarily impart the following information."

"I understand," said Li. He made the disclaimer, and when he was through, he indicated for Erik to turn off the recorder.

"Can I have a glass of water before I start?" Jens went downstairs and returned with a pitcher of water and five glasses. He filled one glass and handed it to Li who drank from it. He indicated to Erik to turn on the recorder.

"I will start with the two large catamaran ships the U.S. use as listening devices up in northern Norway to monitor Russian intelligence regarding the Russian northern fleet in the Bering Sea and Murmansk. These ships, by the way, cost a fortune to build. The intelligence which the ships bring into Bergen on a rotational basis is compromised by Russian agents in Bergen; these agents are Norwegians who are on contractual pay by Russian intelligence. However, the man that the U.S. Embassy in Oslo sends to Bergen each Wednesday to collect a hard copy of this intelligence, hands a copy to his Norwegian friends for which he is well compensated. The Russian Bear is reading your mail America." Li gave the sign for Erik to turn off the recorder. No one in the room made a sound; everyone was watching Li who was taking a sip of water. Li signaled for Erik to turn on the recorder.

"The other problem you have is at your recently upgraded radar station in Bodo, where both the U.S. and Norway spent a lot of money on. The leak there have been going on for about 6 months; it started right after a new Norwegian man was assigned there. A female Captain in the U.S. Air Force stationed there, along with the U.S. contingent, has fallen in love with this new Norwegian man. The romance started in Oslo when both were there on what you call R&R. This young man comes from a very rich and influential Norwegian family. She is letting this Norwegian into the U.S. secure section when she has the night duty and he copies the 24-hour tape while she is in another room collating the hard copies. I don't think she is aware that he copies the tapes. He, in turn, gives her good sex.

The 3rd item concerns a Russian General in charge of intelligence for the NW Russian area to include the border with Norway and the Russian fleet in Murmansk and the Bering Sea. He will be in the area of the border with Norway in August along with his Chief of Staff. They both want to defect to the U.S. and will let the Norwegian command on the border know when and where they want to cross. That's what I have for you now." Li signaled for Erik to stop the recorder. There was not a sound in the room as Li drank from his glass. Erik was the first to speak.

"To be upfront with you, Li, I will bring this information to the U.S. Embassy whom we work closely with and the proper Norwegian authorities. I will classify this information as F-1, which is the highest classification based on previous intelligence which you have given to us. I will not divulge your name or your job until you have made up your mind as to the course of action you have chosen and then with your permission. We here in Norway will do everything to protect this information and yourself. If asked by your people at the Embassy why you are meeting with us, you can tell them we are involved in the Oil and Gas Section of the Norwegian Government, which we are."

"Just so you know, my friend in Sweden who took over the Commerce section at the Embassy, his real job is intelligence and his father is a member of the Politburo in Beijing Standing Committee who answers only to the President. I feel that what he told me is true and we have been like brothers all of our lives. He knows I'm passing the information on; like many of us, he is not happy with the situation in China."

Chapter 10
Overview

The Pandemic spread amongst the countries of the world leaving both rich and poor in a state of shock.

In the more developed countries, the people were told to wear masks and maintain a proper distance from each other. Some businesses were closed or their workers furloughed while others worked from home; this became the norm in large banking and tech industries.

In the United States, schools were closed and students were given educational instruction via computer from their homes. However, this method assumed in error that all students had computers… leaving thousands of students on a prolonged vacation. Churches were told not to administer to their flocks at the expense of heavy fines. Sports venues were canceled or were played to empty stadiums; even the Tokyo 2020 Olympics were canceled.

These draconian measures caused unforeseen problems in many cities and states. Riots prevailed in several cities causing looting and burning of local businesses. Some Mayors and local officials refused to condemn these acts in their cities; from people living in non-affected cities the reluctance of the Mayors and Governors to interfere in these unlawful acts was unimaginable; even some news medias vindicated these violent and unlawful crimes calling them peaceful demonstrations.

2020 was a Presidential election year in the U.S. The Pandemic became politicized and the American population became confused. All of a sudden, so-called experts on the Pandemic were standing in line to espouse their views on TV networks resulting in more confusion and uncertainty among the public.

The annual flu shots normally sponsored by the U.S. Government were barely mentioned. The flu is historically the cause of thousands of deaths in this country. TV stations hammered home each evening the deaths by state caused by the Pandemic, but never mentioned the flu. The news media showed harried hospital doctors and nurses who complained of the lack of hospital beds and equipment. The U.S. President sent two naval hospital ships armed with doctors and nurses - one to New York City and one to California – the two hardest hit places. Each ship had room for a thousand patients. A total of nine (9) patients were sent to the hospital ship in New York and released after 2 weeks; none were sent to the ship in California.

The death total for each state was announced daily and the numbers were staggering. However, the fact that 94% of the people who tested positive were released after approximately 1 week were not well advertised. The people who died initially were mostly those with underlying medical problems. (the same people who succumb to the flu each year – a coincidence?)

There has not been a breakdown of flu cases versus the Pandemic to-date and the news media has not mentioned it.

Confusion has become the norm in the United States.

Chapter 11
Epilogue

Li (*The Red Spade*), received word from his Ambassador that his mother and stepfather had died from the virus. Li contacted his friend at the Chinese Embassy in Sweden who confirmed that the circumstances surrounding their deaths was not due to the virus. Li convinced a friend of his who worked for the Chinese Intelligence Service to become the new "*Red Spade*". Li asked for asylum in the United States and now lives somewhere in the States.

Jens Skogen (Thor) went to work for his father but maintained a close tie to the Norwegian Intelligence Service. His wife, Laura, became an orthopedic surgeon working at the Riks Hospital in Oslo. Laura's brother, Henrik, and his wife, Kirsten, bought Li's house and started a family with Henrik continuing to work with Erik Madsen for the Norwegian Intelligence Service.

Erika Van Hallegen and Lawrence Lee were married at the end of March 2020, at his mother's estate in southern England.

They moved back to the state of Washington. Erika was promoted to Vice-President status at the Boeing Company while her husband supervised the building of their new house in the outskirts of Seattle, WA. In August 2020, Erika gave birth to a healthy boy who was named Lawrence, making both sets of grandparents very happy. Erika's husband, Lawrence, was hired by Boeing as their Marketing Director for Asia.

John and Jean Bergstrom retired after John's release from the hospital. John was the only one of the Governor's five trade reps to survive the virus. They moved to their newly renovated house in Scottsdale, Arizona.

What started out as an accident in a biological research center in Wuhan, China, spread throughout the world leaving few countries untouched. The severity of the pandemic in the United States gave rise to dormant social issues which either because of the virus or the fear of it, caused the semi-takeover of some large cities causing destruction and the collapse of local governments. It turned out that a United States government agency was funding the research in Wuhan, China, in which the experts in epidemiology did not reveal (at least to the public) what had transpired in Wuhan.

Later in the year, only when U.S. laboratories started testing vaccines that proved to be effective, did the news of the U.S. involvement in the research in Wuhan start leaking out piecemeal only to be justified (often denied) by both our government and the people in charge of handing out the funding. Mixed messages continued from our government about the virus which became politicized during the time of the Presidential election. Turmoil fueled by the news media became the norm during the aftermath of the national elections. The supposed news media did not broadcast news but instead editorialized their view depending on which political party's views they backed. Normal life was suspended.

The news media speculated about the future and the new normal awaiting the people. China's hope of destroying the U.S. economy was not in evidence. However, this was a two-edge sword. The stock market players grew richer, but the average citizen grew poorer to the point where the government stepped in and handed out direct cash in the form of checks. In our newly elected government, the word socialism and free everything reared its head. Frustrated old and new left-leaning representatives and senators saw light at the end of the tunnel; only time will validate their hopes.

What will the new normal world look like? Who knows? One thing is obvious, our government needs to do some inward looking. Transparency is needed. The public doesn't need hundreds of experts to include a dentist, with varying views causing confusion.

At the expense of repetitiveness, a few questions need answers:

- Do we as a country hand out large sums of money to a potential enemy for research without oversight of what transpires in their laboratories?
- What happened to the statistical number of flu cases which cause the deaths of thousands of Americans each year, and which our government constantly reminds us each year to get our preventative flu shot?
- Were the flu deaths co-mingled with the virus deaths to make the virus look more ominous, which selective news media outlets hammered home each day to the uninformed American public causing more uncertainty?
- Will we learn from this lost year?

- Will our government be more transparent? Probably not, since we had a mini pandemic here in the U.S. about 9 years ago under the same regime we currently have, which was totally ignored by the then President and our government. Why?

Our Representatives and Senators are quick to use the words "true Democracy" to the rest of the world, holding up our country as the shining example on how it can function.

Are we a Democracy?

No!

We are a Republic.

CPSIA information can be obtained
at www.ICGtesting.com
Printed in the USA
JSHW011009120423
40210JS00004B/118/J

9 781733 314961